Applejack

Emmett Stone

A Black Horse Western

ROBERT HALE · LONDON

ISBN 978-0-7090-9333-6

Robert Hale Limited
Clerkenwell House
Clerkenwell Green
London EC1R 0HT

www.halebooks.com

Typeset by
Derek Doyle & Associates, Shaw Heath
Printed and bound in Great Britain by
CPI Antony Rowe, Chippenham and Eastbourne

CHAPTER ONE

Marshal Rupe Cooley leaned back in his chair on the sidewalk outside his office and looked up to see old Applejack come into view, riding his burro. The oldster came alongside and the marshal touched his hand to his hat.

'Howdy. What are you doin' back in Little Fork?'

The oldster drew to a halt. The donkey's ears twitched as his head turned to look at the marshal with baleful eyes. At the same moment the door to the office opened and the deputy marshal stepped out.

'Hello, old timer,' he said. 'Ain't seen you in a while.'

The oldster gathered phlegm into a ball and shot it in a stream through a hole between his only remaining two front teeth. He seemed to ponder the marshal's words for a few moments till a slow smile stole across his bearded features. He reached into one of his saddle-bags and drew out a pouch, which he opened and shook into the palm of his hand.

'Take a look, Marshal. It's pure gold, and there's plenty more where that come from.'

The marshal tipped his chair forward and stood up. He peered into the oldster's palm.

'Well, I'll be goldanged,' he said.

'On my way back after stakin' my claim,' the oldster said.

'Just be careful who you show that to,' the deputy commented.

'You two run this town real orderly,' Applejack said. 'Ain't seen it so peaceful.'

'I aim to keep it that way,' the marshal replied. 'Baines is right. Once word gets out there's gold in the territory things is likely to change, so for now just keep it to yourself.'

'Sure will, Marshal. No one ain't gonna know nothin' about this except you two, me and old Suky here.'

He turned and rubbed his hand along the donkey's nose.

'Yup, I'll just take me a day's break and then I'm headin' right on back to the Indian River, up above the oxbow lake.'

The marshal shook his head and laughed.

'You never were too discreet, Applejack,' he said. 'You just gone and told us where you found the gold.'

A crease appeared in the oldster's brow.

'Guess you're right,' he said. 'But the Indian River

country is wide and the breaks is rough goin'. Ain't half a dozen people in this here burg ever taken the trouble to ride up there.'

'Let's keep it that way,' the marshal said.

The oldster climbed back into the saddle. Considering he was a small man, his legs reached down almost as far as the ground.

'One other thing,' the marshal said. 'Better check in your gun before you go any further.'

Applejack looked puzzled.

'A new rule I introduced since you've been away,' the marshal said.

The oldster drew a .22 calibre Smith & Wesson from his belt and leaned over to hand it to the marshal.

'You aimin' to stay around for long?' the marshal asked.

'Nope. Not more than one night. Just long enough to get tired of the town, and that won't take long.'

'If you like, you could stay with me and Selma.'

The oldster rubbed his hand across his chin.

'That's real neighbourly of you, Marshal,' he replied. 'But I got ole Suky to think about and she's no more fond of what you might call civilized livin' than I am.'

'You could both share the barn if that would suit you better than a room with a bed and sheets.'

The oldster's face creased in a gesture of distaste.

'Never took a fancy to those high-falutin' things,' he replied. 'I git all kinda scratchy if I've got anythin'' next to me apart from my own skin. But I'll be grateful to pick you up on the offer of the barn. A bed of straw for me and ole Suky might suit just fine.'

'I'll be back after sundown,' the marshal replied, 'but go on over any time. Selma will be glad to see you.'

'You hear that, ole girl?' the oldster addressed the burro. 'Seems like we got us some real nice lodgin's.'

He turned back to the two lawmen.

'See you later,' he said.

The burro trundled off. The marshal grinned and watched Applejack carry on down the street.

'See you later,' Baines said.

He walked away and the marshal, getting to his feet, opened the door of his office and went inside. He slung the gun he had taken from the oldster into a drawer from which he produced a crumpled Wanted poster before shutting and locking it. He held the poster up to the light. It read:

Wanted for murder and robbery.
Cage Drugget.
$1,000 dollar reward for arrest or capture.

'Sure hope he ain't thinkin' of headin' this way,' he murmured. 'Thought I'd seen the last of that no-good coyote.'

He put the poster back into the drawer and, after pacing up and down the room for a few minutes, turned and went back through the door into the street. Walking rapidly, he made his way to the telegraph office. A bell above the door rang as he opened it and went inside.

'Howdy, Marshal,' the man behind the desk said. 'It's like you said. I got another message for you.'

'Figured there might be,' the marshal replied.

The telegraph operator handed him a piece of paper and the marshal scanned its contents. A scowl appeared on his face.

'Everything all right, Mr Cooley?' the telegraph operator asked.

The marshal looked at him and then screwed the paper into a ball.

'I guess it ain't nothin' I can't handle,' he said.

He stepped back outside. The lowering sun was beginning to cast shadows across the street.

It was getting dark when he finally closed the door of the office behind him. Lights were springing out along the main drag and the sounds of merriment billowed out from the Blue Horse saloon. For a moment he contemplated calling in on his way past but contented himself by glancing at the horses tied to the hitchrack. His deputy, Ed Baines, would check out the saloon later. As a general rule there wasn't much trouble these days, at least nothing serious. People got drunk and started fights, there were arguments over card games and women, but things had quieted down since the days he had first taken on the job of marshal. His ban on firearms was the final link in the chain of law enforcement measures which had rendered the town more or less fit for decent folk to live in. Turning away, he continued to walk down the street, nodding to one or two people he passed, and raised his hat to a woman who was just coming out of the grocery store carrying a parcel.

'Gettin' late, Mrs Lake,' he said. 'Can I escort you home? I'm goin' that way.'

'Why, that would be nice,' she replied. 'You can walk me as far as Mr Tench's general store. It should be about closing time and I can pick up Melvin.'

'How is Melvin gettin' on?' the marshal said.

'He gets a bit restless but he'll be fine. Old Sam Tench is just the man to show him the ropes.'

'Melvin's a good boy,' the marshal replied. 'I'm sure he'll do you proud.' They continued to walk together side by side.

'How is Selma?' the woman asked.

'My sister is keepin' well, thank you, ma'am. And yourself?'

'I guess I got nothin' to complain about and my mother is as well as can be expected at her age.'

'You do well to look after her and that boy of yours the way you do.'

They arrived outside the general store.

'Well, I'll be leavin' you now,' Mrs Lake said. 'Why don't you and Selma call round when you get a chance?'

'We surely will,' the marshal replied. He stopped and waited in the street till Mrs Lake was inside the shop. Then he carried on walking till he reached his own house, a similar building but with a dormer roof, which stood near the edge of town. He knocked on the door before opening it and stepping inside.

The place was warmly lit by a couple of oil lamps and a delicious aroma of cooking came from the kitchen. After a moment his sister poked her head round the kitchen door.

'Grub's nearly ready,' she said. 'Come on in and take a seat.'

The marshal loosened his shirt and took off his gun-belt, hanging it over a peg on the wall. He pulled out a chair. The table was covered in a clean white cloth and a vase of flowers stood in the middle of it.

'How are things in town?' his sister called.

'Fine. Sure feel hungry,' he replied. 'I saw old Applejack earlier. I said he could stay in the barn if he liked.'

'In the barn? What's wrong with the spare room?'

'Ain't nothin' wrong with it but you know how the old goat is. Ain't you seen him yet?'

'Nope, he hasn't stopped by.'

'I thought he'd have been here by now.'

While they ate they exchanged the usual pleas-antries, but the marshal couldn't help feeling that something was wrong. It was unlike Applejack to turn down the chance of a good meal. When they were finished and the dinner table was cleared, he strolled to the porch and leaned against the veranda rail. After a few moments Selma came to join him.

'You're still thinking about Applejack,' she said. 'He's a cussed old devil. Like as not he's either tucked between the sheets in a hotel room or he's left town and set up camp somewhere.'

'He certainly wouldn't be stayin' in no hotel,'

Cooley replied. 'He might have left town but I don't think so.'

His sister pressed close to him and he put his arm round her.

'Is there somethin' else?' she said. 'You seem distracted.'

'It don't amount to anythin' much,' he replied, keeping the focus of attention on Applejack, 'but when he came ridin' by he told me he'd struck gold. He said he'd staked his claim and was on his way back to the Indian River.'

'He told you where it was?'

'Yup. Somewhere above the oxbow lake. He showed me some of the dust he'd panned. Looked real enough to me. Trouble is, he probably showed it to a lot of other folks too.'

'That would be like him,' Selma replied. 'He's always been too trustin'.'

The marshal looked down at his sister.

'I reckon I might just take a walk back into town,' he said. 'See if I can find out what's happened to Applejack.'

He walked back into the house, took down his gun-belt and strapped it round his waist.

'I won't be long,' he said.

'Just you be careful,' Selma replied.

The marshal made his way back towards the centre of town. A wind had sprung up and the night had grown cool. From somewhere a dog began to bark. The main street of town was completely deserted and all remaining activity was concentrated at the Blue Horse saloon. Some of the horses that had been fastened to the hitchrack had gone but there were still a number remaining. With a glance in their direction, the marshal stepped on to the boardwalk and pushed through the batwings. The smoke-filled room was quiet; a few people sat at tables just drinking or playing at cards and a couple of men he recognized from neighbouring ranches were standing at the bar. As he moved to the bar rail some of the card players looked up and acknowledged his presence with a nod. The men at the bar turned and one of them said, 'Howdy'. The marshal's quick eyes observed that none of them was wearing a gun.

'Good to see you, Marshal,' the bartender said. 'Care for a drink?'

'Nope. Thought I'd just glance in as I was passin' by.'

The bartender continued wiping a glass, which he then placed back on a shelf.

'Don't suppose you've seen old Applejack?' the marshal said.

Reflected in the mirror of the bar, the marshal thought he detected a quick glance pass between the two cowboys. The bartender appeared entirely unmoved.

'Sure,' he said. 'He was in earlier.'

'What time was that?'

The barman shrugged.

'About five.'

'How long did he stay?'

'He had a couple of drinks and then went. Not long.'

'He didn't say anythin' about where he was goin'?'

Again the barman shook his head.

'What is this, Marshal? The old goat ain't gone and robbed the bank or somethin'?'

The two at the bar laughed but it sounded hollow to the marshal's ears.

'Not this time,' he said.

He glanced at the ranch-hands.

'Some of you boys leave early?'

The elder of the two put his glass on the counter.

'Sure.'

He turned to his friend.

'Come on,' he said. 'I guess it's about time we were gettin' back too.'

'Tell Starr Schandler I'll stop by one of these days,' the marshal said. 'Ain't been out to the Triangle S in a whiles.'

The two left and the marshal soon followed. He had learned nothing definite but he had a feeling there was something they had left unsaid. He carried on walking in the direction he had been following before going into the Blue Horse till he arrived at the end of the street. A few ramshackle buildings tailed off into the darkness of the open country across which the dusty road lay like a dropped ribbon, glimmering faintly in the starlight. The marshal stood with his arms folded across his chest. He still had an uneasy feeling. He reached inside a pocket for his pouch of tobacco and felt the crumpled telegram. Cage Drugget had been let out of jail. It was confirmed. That didn't mean Drugget would necessarily think of making his way to Little Fork, but the marshal couldn't help but think it was a fair bet. After all, he had been responsible for capturing Drugget and putting him behind bars. The gunslinger had sworn to get even and Cooley had no reason to think that a spell in prison would bring about a change of mind. The man was a ruthless killer and it would only be common sense to prepare for the worst. And now, to add to his unease, the oldster had failed to show up at his house and he had an uncomfortable feeling that it was not because he had changed his plans. He built a smoke and pondered the situation. For the time being there wasn't much he could do. He decided to leave it till the morning. He would take that ride out to the Triangle S and keep his eyes open for any clues as to the oldster's disappearance as he rode. Finishing the cigarette, he turned on his heel and walked back through the town. On the way he stepped into the only hotel on the slim chance that the oldster might have checked in, but as he expected, there was nothing in the register and the hotel clerk had not seen him. Maybe Applejack was camped out on the prairie, but Cooley doubted that was the case.

Next morning Cooley was awake early, but early as he was, his sister was up before him.

'I thought you'd appreciate a good breakfast before you set off,' she said.

15

'How did you know I was leavin' early? I never said anythin'.'

'You came back last night disappointed at not having found old Applejack. I kinda figured you wouldn't wait long.'

She placed a plate of bacon and eggs on the table.

'I figured I'd take a look out towards the Triangle S, maybe pay Schandler a visit while I'm doin' it.'

Selma gave her brother a searching glance.

'Watch what you're doing,' she said. 'There's something about Schandler I don't like.'

'I know what you mean. Some of his boys were in the Blue Horse last night. I got a feelin' they knew somethin' they weren't sayin'.'

Selma left the room and returned with a pot of coffee.

'Are you takin' Baines along with you?'

'Nope. Figured I'd leave him behind to keep an eye on things here. It don't take two of us to handle Starr Schandler.'

She poured out a mug of black coffee.

'Like I say, just be careful,' she said.

'I always am,' he replied.

He didn't mention anything about the telegram or Cage Drugget because he didn't want to worry her any more than was usual.

Across the hot and lonely landscape, a wagon crawled. Sitting high next to one another were a man past his middle years and a young woman.

'I figure we must be over half way to Harpington

16

now,' the man said.

'I don't care how far it is,' she replied. 'I'm just enjoying the ride.'

'I hope I've done the right thing,' he said. 'After all, what do we know of life on a farm?'

'Of course you've done the right thing, as you put it. Besides, it wasn't just you made the decision. We talked it over plenty of times. I wanted to leave Layton and the general store even more than you.'

The woman smiled at her father and then let her gaze wander. They had come through some rough broken country nearer to the river, but now it was richer and grassier, sweeping away to some far blue hills.

'If we had stayed in Layton,' she continued, 'we might never have seen views like this.'

They lapsed into silence. The horses plodded along, making an effort as the land rose. Their tails flicked to keep off the flies. Suddenly, outlined against the sky, a group of horsemen appeared. They both saw them at the same time.

'Ain't come across anybody for a whiles,' the man said. 'I guess they must be some riders from one of the nearby ranches.'

'We've seen a few cattle,' his daughter remarked. 'Maybe they've come to round them up.'

They watched as the riders came down the sloping ground ahead of them. There were four of them, strung out and approaching at a steady canter. The man was preparing to give them a welcome when something about them caused him concern. He glanced sideways at his daughter.

'Go inside the wagon,' he said.

She returned his look and was about to say something when he repeated what he had said.

'Get inside the wagon!'

There was no ignoring his peremptory tones. With a last glance at the approaching horsemen, she got out of her seat and climbed into the canvas-covered interior.

As she did so, her father brought the wagon to a halt. One of the horsemen drew up but the others continued round the sides of the wagon so that he couldn't see what was happening towards the back. He looked up at the stationary rider.

'Howdy,' he said.

By way of reply, the horseman spat into the dust. The wagon driver leaned out to see what might be happening behind him. Two of the riders appeared to be interfering with the wagon cover and his fears were confirmed when he saw a flash of metal and the tearing sounds of canvas being ripped.

'Hey, wait a minute!' he began, turning back to the man on the horse beside him, but before he could say anything else the man had drawn his six-gun and fired at him at point blank range. He felt a shattering pain in his chest but succeeded in getting to his feet before another shot sent him flying sideways from the wagon seat to land with a thud on the grass. A scream of terror rose from the wagon as the two attackers leered at the frightened woman inside. She scrambled for the tail-board but even as she reached it the wagon cover was drawn aside by another rider. As she climbed awkwardly over the side, he dropped from his horse and seized her, but she managed to push him aside as she turned and began to run towards the front of the wagon. In an instant he was upon her, seizing her by the shoulder and tearing her blouse. For a few moments they struggled; she felt her fingernails scratch their way down the man's cheek and with a cry his grip on her loosened. Tearing herself free, she only succeeded in running into one of the other men. She fell heavily. In an instant the two men had flung themselves upon her, dragging her back to her feet. One of them had his hand across her mouth and she bit down hard. He drew it back sharply and then brought it down on her head. The force of it sent her staggering to the ground again. She started to crawl and through the pain that was engulfing her she heard the sounds of hoofs and someone shouting.

'What the hell are you doin'? One of you get over here and help Quinn unhitch these horses while the other starts unloadin' the wagon.'

Through mists of pain and fear she glanced aside at her attackers. Even in her distress she couldn't help but notice how they seemed to jump at the man's orders.

'Sure thing, boss,' one of them said.

She turned her aching head to see the horse and its rider disappear round the corner of the wagon. She still expected the men to renew their assault but nothing happened. Instead they moved away and she continued to inch her way towards some bushes. As she edged forwards they seemed to get no nearer but after what seemed an age she succeeded in reaching them and dragged herself into their shelter. Shortly afterwards sheets of flames rose from the wagon, but she was no longer conscious to observe them.

Cooley had intended setting off early, but decided to check once more in town to see if old Applejack had put in an appearance or if anybody had seen him. He could have saved himself the effort. He called in at the marshal's office to advise Baines about what he was doing and enjoin him to keep his eyes and ears open for any news of the oldster. By the time he had finished, it was relatively late before he finally climbed into the saddle and rode away. As he went he looked about him for any trace of Applejack and kept checking the ground for sign of the oldster's passing. The day slipped by without him seeing anything of significance.

When the horse reached the crest of a low rise, Cooley dismounted and drew a telescope from his saddle-bags. Even before putting the instrument to his eye he had discerned something which didn't seem to fit. He tugged the horse's rein and pulled it back from the edge of the plateau. Then he got to his knees and crawled over the rim to lie flat. Taking care that no sunlight reflected from the lens of the telescope, he pointed it towards what he had seen. For a moment the eyepiece wavered before it came to rest on what had alarmed him. It was a burned-out wagon and, lying next to it, what appeared to be a body. Getting to his feet, he swung back into the saddle and let the horse pick its slow way down to the foot of the hill. The ground began to level off. As they got nearer the wagon and its remains, the horse pricked up its ears.

What was left of the wagon lay in a little hollow. Cooley dismounted and walked the last few yards. As he approached, he brushed away swarms of flies. The remains were those of an elderly man. He had been shot twice. Cooley looked about him. From the sign that was left, it was clear that a number of riders were involved. He was puzzled because the place had been peaceful of late. Then he had a thought which brought him up sharply: Cage Drugget. He remembered some of the crimes of which Drugget had been suspected but never found guilty. Drugget had recently been released from jail and the marshal had a feeling he could be on his way to seek revenge. Could Drugget have got this far already? Could he have been responsible? If so, he had teamed up with at least a couple of others of his breed.

He turned back to the body. Who was he? He felt his stomach turn in revulsion. His instinct was to try and bury him, but he had no equipment. His considerations were suddenly broken into by what seemed to be a faint groaning sound. He tensed and his hand automatically moved to the Colt in his holster. He went down on one knee, turning his head in the direction of the sound. He listened carefully, but there was no repetition and he was beginning to

21

think he must have been imagining things. Maybe it was the horse or the movement of some creature in the grass. Then it came again – so softly that might have been easily missed had everything not been so quiet and his own senses stretched and alert. For another moment he remained confused. His first thought was that it might be the perpetrators returning to the scene. Then it suddenly became obvious that it must be a survivor.

Quickly he got to his feet and, with his gun in his hand, began to move cautiously in the direction of the sound. He could see nothing. He was moving away from the immediate vicinity and was beginning to think he had got the direction wrong. It would be an easy mistake to make. Then he heard it again, a gasping moan, but this time it was louder. There were some low bushes this side of the hollow and the sound was surely coming from there. He pushed though the little barrier, fearful of what he might find, and then he saw a figure lying there, partially protected by the brush. As he got near he could see that it was a partially clothed female. She was lying on her side. Quickly he knelt down and carefully turned her over, using his arms to cushion her head. Blood was matted in her hair from an ugly blow to the skull, but from a cursory look he could see no other obvious wounds. Any further examination was cut short when, unexpectedly, her eyes opened and she looked into his face. At first she looked bemused and then an expression of panic and fear began to spread across her features.

'It's all right,' he said. 'I won't harm you. I found you here.'

'Who are you?' she breathed.

'I'm a United States marshal, but don't worry about that now. How do you feel?'

'My head hurts,' she said.

'You've got quite a bad scalp wound. You've been struck by something.' For a few moments she was silent, as if trying to assimilate the information.

'How long have I been here?'

'Can't rightly say.'

He could hazard a good guess, but he didn't want to say anything about what else he had found. It seemed as if she divined his thoughts.

'What about my father?' she asked.

He felt awkward.

'I'm sorry,' was all he could say.

She seemed to understand, and for a while neither of them spoke. What was she thinking? Whatever it was, she began to show signs of animation.

'Do you feel pain anywhere else?' he asked.

'I don't think so. I feel stiff and my leg hurts but otherwise I'm OK.'

'Let's see if we can move you,' he said. 'Do you think you're strong enough to try and stand?'

She nodded and with his help began to struggle to her feet, wincing a few times as she did so. When she finally stood without his support, she suddenly seemed to become aware of her state of undress and clutched what was left of her blouse about her.

'Do you feel able to walk?' he asked.

'Yes,' she replied and attempted a few stumbling steps. Then she started to sway and he stepped forward to put his arm around her shoulders.

'Thanks,' she whispered, 'I think I might need your assistance.'

Together they walked slowly back towards the hollow. He was attempting to guide her away from the wagon and the remains of its occupant, but she seemed to become aware of this and halted.

'It's all right,' she said. 'I want to see. I can deal with it. But I'll still need your help.'

He had no choice. When they reached the wagon she paused and then asked him to help her over to where the body lay.

'I'm really sorry,' he repeated.

She seemed to be calm but then she began to weep and laid her head on his shoulder. When she finally drew away, she continued to look down in silence.

'Come on,' she said. 'There's nothing anyone can do for him now.'

'There's something I can do,' he replied, forgetting his first intentions. 'I can try and give him some decent kind of burial.'

'We need to think about ourselves,' she said, and he was struck by the practical turn of her mind. Something else registered with him but he only became aware of it later; the way in which she had included them both.

'I won't just leave him,' he said, and she seemed too exhausted now to demur. He walked her back to where he had left the horse and helped her to sit down. Pulling out his water container, he gave it to her, advising her to drink slowly.

'You'll be all right here for a while,' he said. 'Just give me a shout if you need to. I won't be far.'

He turned away, not sure what he was intending to do. He could leave the corpse, return to town with the woman and arrange for the undertaker to come out and collect it. But that would all take time and he felt a strange responsibility not to leave the body exposed. But what could he do? Even if he had a pick or a spade, it would take a long time to bury the remains. He began to drag the body below the rim of the hollow beneath the bushes where he managed to dislodge sufficient earth to cover it thinly. Glancing up from the work and wiping sweat from his brow, he saw the woman approaching.

'You should rest,' he said.

'There'll be time for that,' she replied.

'Help me cover him over,' he said.

Together they pulled out some branches and laid them over the top of the shallow grave. It was little enough but it was better then nothing. When they had finished they hesitated for a moment. There should be some sort of ceremony. Finally, with bowed head, he intoned some words he remembered from childhood:

'*Shall we gather at the river, the beautiful, the beautiful river.*'

She seemed to be familiar with it and her voice rose with his.

'*Soon we'll reach the shining river, soon our pilgrimage will cease.*'

Dusk was descending. The sun was a red orb balanced on the horizon.

'I think it's time we got out of here,' he said. 'We'll ride until we find somewhere to camp.'

He did not intend riding far. He had thought about returning to town but the girl was obviously in need of time to recover from her ordeal before facing anybody. He didn't know if he was doing the right thing, but it seemed to him the best idea would be to make camp not too far from where her father was buried and give her time to grieve. Quite apart from that, he felt strangely tired himself, and it wasn't just the exertion of burying the old man. The horse, too, could do with some rest; it would have to carry the two of them. Carefully and with some difficulty he helped the woman into the saddle and then swung up behind her. At a touch on the reins the horse moved forward. The sky was filling with the first pale stars and the evening air was cool. With his arms around the woman to keep her steady, and with the regular rhythm of the animal's tread, he found it difficult to keep his eyes open and not fall asleep. He let the horse find its own way.

A slice of moon had risen, and by its light and the light of the stars he peered into the darkness looking for signs that might indicate a pool or a watercourse. They hadn't been riding far in this fashion when he saw the outline of trees and decided that this was the place they must halt for the rest of the night. As they approached, Cooley began to discern the clear, unmistakable babble of running water and they emerged on the banks of a stream, which he guessed was a tributary of the Indian River.

'Whoa boy!' he called, and the sound must have awoken the woman because she began to stir and looked round at him.

'Where are we?' she said, bemused.

'We'll camp here for the night,' he replied, climbing wearily down from the horse and then helping her to dismount. Settling her on the ground, he began to look for materials to start a fire.

'I can help,' she said.

'Take it steady,' he replied. 'I'm not sure you're in a condition to do anything just yet.'

'No,' she replied. 'I'm feeling a bit better. It'll do me good to be doing something.'

'If you're sure you can manage, you might try gettin' some water while I build a fire.'

'Are you sure that would be a good idea?' she asked.

'What do you mean?'

'Might it not give away our position? Whoever shot my father might still be about.'

She was right; chances were that they would be safe, but it would be foolish to take any risks.

'It could get a mite cold,' he replied. 'I guess we'll just have to make ourselves as comfortable as we can without a fire.'

'The first thing I'm going to do,' she said, 'is go down into that stream and freshen up. I must look terrible. I'll get us some water at the same time.'

She allowed him to help her as she struggled to her feet, but then she waved him aside.

'I won't be long,' she said and, taking the canteen she took from the saddle-bags, walked steadily away.

While she was gone he undid his belongings and made sure that the horse was settled for the night. Then he looked to see what they might eat. Without a fire, it would have to be jerky and biscuits washed down with water. He would have given a lot for some strong, hot coffee. The main problem would be keeping sufficiently warm without a fire. From behind his saddle he had unloaded his bed-roll, blankets and slicker, and by the time she came back he had made things tolerably comfortable. Hearing her footsteps, he turned and was immediately struck by the change in her appearance. She had done what she could to wash away the dirt and blood, and now he saw for the first time how beautiful she was. Her dark short hair framed an oval face and her body, though thin, was finely shaped and curved in the right places. Water dripped from her and she was shivering.

'You need to get out of those things,' he said, throwing her the blanket. She looked hesitant.

'I'm sorry if I seem to be a bit forward,' he added, 'but we can't afford the niceties. If you don't get out of those wet things you might catch a chill. The situation we're in, it's all about survival. Give me a shout when you're decent.'

Feeling agitated, he went down and washed

himself in the stream. She was a beautiful woman, all right. Things could get decidedly awkward with her in tow. When he came back she had the blanket wrapped around her and had stopped shaking. He sat down beside her.

'Just to get things straight,' he said, 'I'm not sure how to put this, but you've nothing to fear from me. We've got ourselves into a situation and for the time bein' we'll just have to manage it.'

She nodded.

'I understand and agree entirely,' she said. 'And I don't feel afraid of you. Is that strange? Maybe it's because you're a lawman. I don't know, but I guess I owe my life to you. If you hadn't have turned up, I suppose I would have just lain there until, well, I would have just lain there.'

She paused, thoughtful.

'That was pretty lucky you happening along.'

'Perhaps I'd better explain what I'm doin' here,' he said. 'I'm lookin' for someone. He's an old timer. Folks call him Applejack.'

'That's a funny name,' she said. 'Why are you looking for him? Has he done something wrong?'

Smiling, he stretched his arms and yawned.

'Nope, it ain't nothin' like that. To tell you the truth, that's a real good question. He might be an old timer, but I guess he can look after himself. The thing is, he was supposed to be stayin' with me and Selma but he didn't show up. He's kinda disappeared.'

'Selma?' she said. 'Is she your wife?'

'My sister,' he replied.

He couldn't help yawning again and he could see the tiredness written across the woman's features.

'Lady,' he said, 'I guess I'm just too tired to go into this right now. I need sleep and so do you. Let's leave it till tomorrow.'

She shrugged.

'That's OK with me,' she replied.

He knew that someone should keep watch. Finding a spot a short distance away, he wrapped himself in his slicker and placed his firearms within easy reach.

'By the way,' he called, 'I guess we'd better get on name terms. I'm Rupe Cooley.'

'And I'm Belinda,' she replied. 'Belinda Chesterton.'

'Nice to meet you. Goodnight, Belinda,' he replied.

CHAPTER TWO

Cooley awoke with the morning sun beating down on him. At first he was confused, then the events of the previous day came back and he was immediately on his feet. The woman was still sleeping, though the sun was quite high. He went down to the stream and waded into the water. When he returned she was up and about.

'We've slept late,' he said. 'Let's eat quickly and get out of here. I think we might be pushing our luck already.'

'Which way do we go?' she replied.

'I guess we'd better get you safe to town,' he said.

The look she gave him was less than enthusiastic.

'What about your friend, Mr Applejack?'

'He can wait. The important thing is to get you somewhere safe.'

They ate quickly, an unappetizing meal of jerky and water from the stream, the same as the previous evening. Then they mounted the roan, the woman in front and Cooley behind. At first they were both silent, straining their eyes to see across the empty landscape, beginning to shimmer now in the heat. The stream lay on their right, and they followed a line of stunted willows. Cooley again let the horse go at its own speed, watching for gopher holes near at hand and for any signs of danger ahead. They were both silent till Belinda spoke.

'What are you thinking?' she said.

'Nothing much,' he lied.

'I haven't had a chance to thank you for rescuing me.'

'No need,' he said. 'I'm just glad I happened by when I did.'

She looked ahead again before turning back.

'I've been thinking. Why do you think they let me go?'

'What do you mean?'

'Those men. They could have killed me.' She hesitated. 'Or, you know, other things.'

Cooley experienced a surge of something inside him. He was surprised at the depth of relief he felt.

'I didn't like to say anything,' he replied, 'about what happened.'

'We were heading for a place called Harpington,' she said. 'My father ran a store in Layton. We got by but then we heard from my uncle offering a share of a farm. We were on our way. Maybe we were foolish to travel alone, but we didn't think we'd have trouble, certainly not something like this. Not till yesterday.'

Her voice broke and she began to sob.

'It wasn't your fault,' Cooley said. 'How were you to know?'

'I guess we must have been stupid. If we'd have taken thought, this might never have happened.'

'What did happen?' Cooley asked.

'There were four of them. We didn't think . . . I was in the wagon – it was horrible. Two of them grabbed me. I tried to fight them off. All I remember after that is being on the ground outside the wagon and trying to crawl away. I don't recall anything more till you came along.'

'You did well,' Cooley replied. 'I guess you were lucky. They didn't concern themselves about you. Maybe they were simply concentrating on getting their booty. You must have been sufficiently aware to find that one place among the bushes where you were concealed.'

Again they felt silent. He was about say something further, when suddenly he tensed. Away off in the distance he could see a vague smudge against the horizon. He guessed it was dust. It could be caused by several things – buffalo, wagons even – but it could also be Belinda's attackers. He wasn't going to take any chances. Gently he spurred the horse to a faster pace.

'What is it?' Belinda asked as she became aware that they were moving more quickly.

'Look over to your left,' he said.

'I don't see anything.'

'There's something raising dust – can't tell how far off, but it could be the men who attacked you.'

She looked again, and this time she too detected the distant smear.

'What are we going to do?' she asked.

'I don't know – what cover there is will be along the stream. If we can get into it at this point, it might help conceal our tracks.'

So saying, he pulled on the reins to turn the horse towards the water. The stream was quite a lot wider at this point, but the gently sloping banks provided no obstacle to the horse's progress. Cooley couldn't tell how deep it was towards the centre. Where the roan entered the water it was shallow and he let it splash through. With anxious eyes he kept turning to look in the direction of the tell-tale dust cloud. Crossing the river would make little difference, but he decided it might be worth a try. The flow of the water was comparatively slow here on the flat plain.

'Hold on tight!' he yelled, 'I'm going to cross to the other side. I think we'll be OK, but there's no real telling how deep the water gets in the middle.'

He urged his mount further into the water. It was still quite shallow, beginning to lap around the horse's belly. Then the horse gave a sudden lurch as the ground slipped away beneath its feet and it was swimming in deeper water, the river's flow carrying it downstream as it struggled to maintain direction. Further ahead and off to their left stood a patch of willows, their leaves trailing into the water, and Cooley set his sights on them as his target. They seemed to be doing well. The current was not too strong and the horse was making good progress. Just a bit further and they might strike solid ground again. Once the horse's hoofs made contact with the river-bed they should be safe. The opposite bank was getting nearer and he was feeling confident when disaster struck. Suddenly they were caught in an unexpected eddy of water. Cooley was concentrating all his efforts on guiding and encouraging the roan when without warning, Belinda gave a cry and slipped off the horse's wet back into the water. For a brief moment he tried to catch her, but then she was out of reach.

'Swim!' he shouted uselessly.

She began to flail her arms. He didn't know if she could swim or not, or how well. He tried to turn the horse in the current, but it was no use – he couldn't reach her. He thought she was moving ahead, but the current, although not strong, was sufficient to carry her away from him. With a despairing look at her head bobbing in the water, he concentrated on getting to the other side of the stream, cursing himself for having made the decision to cross, and also for not holding on to her better. The water was deeper than he had anticipated; they seemed to have been in it for an age but in fact it was only a matter of a few minutes. With a sensation of baffled relief, Cooley sensed that the horse was moving forward more confidently, and the next moment it was no longer swimming but on its feet again. Without further mishap it moved through the shallower water until it came struggling up the opposite bank, which was a little steeper here, water streaming down its sides.

They had come out just above the stretch of willows, and quickly Cooley urged the tired roan through the trees and along the river-bank, searching desperately for a sign that Belinda had managed to reach safety. Hard as he looked he could not see her either on the river-bank or in mid-stream. He pulled the horse to a halt and searched the river with desperate eyes but failed to detect her. He had been right about their pursuers; they were still quite distant but closing fast. Had they seen him? He couldn't be sure, but they certainly seemed to be riding with a purpose. He strained his eyes, but it was impossible to tell how many there were – certainly more than four. What was he to do? He was caught in two minds. His overriding impulse was to search for Belinda but he realized that if the gang were to catch sight of him, he would be in deep trouble. His best chance seemed to be to hide himself among the willows and rushes which lined the banks of the river at this juncture. There was no point in riding further. It was unlikely there would be any better cover and the horse was, in any event, exhausted.

Quickly he slid from the saddle and led the horse among the trees. Then he took cover himself, crouching down behind the trunk of a cypress and some low bushes. Anxiously he surveyed the scene on the opposite bank. He would have used the telescope, but was afraid it might glint in the sunlight and give away his position. He checked his rifle and laid his Colts on the earth beside him where he could easily take them up, hoping it would not come to shooting. If it did, he knew the odds were not good. At least he could take some of them with him.

The group of horsemen was getting quite close now. He counted eight, loping at a steady pace in the direction of the river. Suddenly one of the lead riders veered and brought his horse to a halt, holding up his hand for the others to do likewise. He made a gesture and then pointed in the direction of the river about a mile and a half from where Cooley was hiding. Sure enough the party then began to move towards the river. When they were closer the man, who appeared to be the leader, slid from his saddle and began to examine the ground. With a sickening thud in his stomach Cooley guessed that they had picked up the trail of the roan. They would be able to follow it along the river, and it would not be hard for them to work out at which point he had entered the water. The rider remounted and the whole party moved on at a steadier pace. Cooley was straining his eyes to get a look at the man's face. He was still at some distance, but Cooley was pretty sure he recognized Cage Drugget.

He knew now he would have no choice but to fight them. What were his chances? He was in good cover and would have the advantage of surprise. They knew he was somewhere near, but might not guess the exact spot. He decided that his best option would be to open up and let them have it the moment they entered the river. Some of them, at least, probably knew the river better than he did. It might not present the same problems for them that it had for him. For a moment he entertained a hope that they might decide not to go into the water at this point but search for a fording place further along. He watched them now with unwavering attention. Let them carry on, he prayed, but he knew it was to no avail when they stopped again and the leader began to point towards the opposite bank. They had reached the point where he had spurred the roan into the water. He was hoping now that the horse would not make a noise and give away his position, losing him the advantage. Suddenly it didn't matter, because one of the riders raised his rifle and loosed a shot which tore into the foliage above Cooley's head. They must have seen him. Other men began to fire. He raised his rifle to his shoulder and drew a bead on the nearest rider. They were moving down the bank, their horses taking their first steps into the water. Cooley felt his palm sweating but there was no time now to delay. Holding his arm steady, he pulled the trigger and as the smoke cleared, saw the man fall backwards into the water. The others stopped and hesitated, unsure for a moment whether to go forward or back. Without hesitation Cooley fired again and this time another rider slipped sideways, seeming to hold his position for a few seconds before sliding into the shallows.

The rest of the party now started to yell and a few urged their horses towards the deeper water. A couple of them turned and began to seek the river-bank. Cooley was not thinking now. The adrenalin had caught him and he was acting instinctively. He

reloaded and snapped off more shots, oblivious of
the bullets that tore into the trees and bushes all
around him. He had the clearer view and at this
range, and with his skill, it was almost impossible to
miss. Two more riders collapsed into the water, their
horses snorting and rearing. A horse went down – he
could not tell if its rider was hit but he could see
blood streaming from a hip wound to another rider.
One of the riders reaching the middle of the river
seemed to be swept away by the current. A few scattered shots continued to come in his direction, but
they were wild and did not offer much threat. The
remaining gunmen had reached the further bank
now and were riding away. Soon they were out of
range, retracing their steps upstream.

Cooley suddenly felt breathless and both elated
and downcast at the same time. He had beaten them
off for the moment, but he knew they would be back.
Next time they might even have reinforcements. He
realized that his best plan might be to stay put. He
had a strong position, as events had proved. He
could see bodies of both men and horses in the shallows on the other side of the stream and he guessed
that others would have been carried away by the
current. But he felt an urge now to get away, and an
overwhelming need to find out what had happened
to Belinda.

Without further hesitation he climbed into the
saddle and reined his horse along the bank, taking
care to use what cover he could. His eyes searched
the river and the river-banks on both sides for

Belinda, for any sign of her. What could have happened to her? He didn't want to admit to himself the possibility that she had drowned. He tensed. Ahead there was some sort of snag in the river – a log that had become jammed. Across it there lay what appeared from a distance to be an inert figure. Belinda? Cooley wasn't sure whether he wanted it to be her or not. It wasn't moving. When he got closer, however, he could see that it was the body of one of the gunmen.

He had ridden down the river for a fair distance. He was now debating with himself whether to go on or return in the direction from which he had come in case he had missed her. In the end he decided to carry on for the time being, putting distance between himself and the gunmen. Still he could see no sign of Belinda. He began to lose heart. She must have drowned. She was somewhere beneath the water, perhaps held in a snag like the one which had trapped the dead gunman but under the surface. He had been foolish to suppose she might survive and he might find her. He had been even more foolish to attempt the crossing in the first place. He felt guilty now, as though everything was his fault. A chill had begun to descend over the river. Then, just as he was sinking into a mood of black depression, he was jerked back to awareness. On the opposite bank he could make out a figure. It was gesticulating towards him; his first thought was for Cage Drugget and he reached for his rifle. Then his heart thumped and he could see that it was not any gunman but a female figure: it was Belinda. A gust of wind brought her voice to him above the sounds of the water and he called back as loud as he could.

'Belinda! Belinda!'

He dropped the rifle and spurred the horse forward, feeling a new energy flood his being as he negotiated his way into the shallows. He splashed his way across the stream as Belinda ran into the water to meet him. As he approached her he leaped down and then they were in one another's arms. For a few moments they held each other close before they moved apart to scramble up the river-bank. When they were clear of the water they looked at one another, both feeling a little foolish.

'I'll just get the horse,' Cooley said brusquely.

He waded back into shallows and, taking the roan's bridle, led it out of the water. By the time he had hobbled it, Belinda had recovered her equilibrium.

'That was a close thing,' she said. 'I heard shooting from down the river. What happened?'

Briefly, Cooley recounted his exchange of fire with the men who had pursued them. He didn't mention the name Cage Drugget.

'What I don't quite understand,' he said, 'is why they were so keen to follow us.'

Belinda shivered, although her clothes were almost dry.

'Anyway, what happened to you?' Cooley said.

'When I slipped into the water my clothes carried me down but luckily I can swim quite well,' she

41

replied. 'I began to make for the opposite bank but the current was too strong. For a time I lay on my back and let the river carry me. When I felt I was in shallower water, I began to use my arms again. Finally my feet struck solid ground and I was able to reach the river-bank. I was exhausted. I must have lain for a considerable time while the sun dried me. When I recovered, I started walking but after a while I began to suspect I was going in the wrong direction. I turned and began to walk back. I had just about given up hope of finding you when I saw you.'

It was obvious that the sense of relief had been mutual.

When she had finished, Cooley began to look about him, trying to get his bearings. His intention had been to get back to town but it seemed to him now that the Triangle S would be nearer. With Cage Drugget and his men in the vicinity, it might make more sense to head for the ranch. Quickly, he explained his plan to Belinda.

'Sounds fine by me,' she replied.

They mounted up once more and set off, travelling along a well marked trail until eventually, Cooley turned the horse off on a narrower track. They appeared to have the range to themselves, but as they continued they began to see cattle browsing.

'Some of 'em should be Triangle S stock,' Cooley called. 'We must be gettin' close to the boundary. Let's take a closer look.'

They rode across to where some of the longhorns were gathered in a bunch. Cooley slid from the roan.

'Yup,' he said after finding the distinctive elongated letter S. He looked at some of the others.

'It's a bit strange,' he said. 'Usually there would be different brands. This was open range. Nobody bothered much till roundup. These cattle all seem to be marked with the same Triangle S brand.'

'What does that mean?' Belinda asked.

Cooley looked up sharply.

'I don't know,' he said, 'but somethin' ain't right.'

He bent down to take a further look before remounting. He touched his spurs to the horse's flanks, but they hadn't gone very far when they saw a bunch of riders coming towards them. Cooley's first thought was that they might be some of Drugget's men but even if they were, there was nothing he could do about it. He glanced at Belinda. Considering all she had gone through, she didn't seem to show any obvious signs of fear. As the riders came closer and drew to a halt, they spread out so they were blocking the trail. The man who appeared to be their leader wore batwing leather chaps with built-in holsters over which his right hand hovered. He stared hard at them for some time before he finally spoke.

'Turn right round,' he growled. 'This is private land.'

'As far as I remember, it's open range.'

'Was. Once.'

'We didn't see any sign.'

'You want a sign, I'll give you one.'

In a flash he had drawn his gun and was pointing

it at Cooley.

'I suggest you just turn right round and ride back where you came from,' he barked.

'Now just take it easy,' Cooley said. 'As you can see, we've had a bit of trouble. Figured we'd get to the Triangle S and pick up a horse.'

The man showed no sign of relenting. The situation was getting more awkward by the moment and Cooley didn't want to put Belinda in further jeopardy. He turned to her. 'Let's do as the man wants,' he said.

They began to ride away.

'The name's Quinn,' the man called after them. 'Remember it and make sure there's not a next time because if there is, I can guarantee it'll be your last.'

They retraced their steps, not looking back till they had covered some distance. When Cooley did turn, the riders were still straggled across the trail watching their retreat.

'A nice welcome,' Belinda said.

'Yes, but I think another courtesy call might be in order,' Cooley replied.

He was feeling confused. The men looked mean enough to be riding with Drugget, but they seemed to be Triangle S hands. He hadn't seen any of them before. What had they been doing before accosting him and Belinda? Could they have been involved in running off cattle from other ranches so that only Triangle S stock remained?

As they rode, Cooley's senses were alert for any sign of Cage Drugget. He thought hard about the dif-

44

ferent possible trails he might follow that led into
town in order to best avoid the gunman and his
gang. He knew the area well so felt reasonably confident that they could reach town in safety. Belinda
had fallen silent and he made no attempt at conversation. The roan was doing well under its double
burden but Cooley regretted not having made for
town in the first place. If he had, he would have
avoided the incident at the river. He was thinking
again about what he had mentioned to Belinda. Why
had Drugget bothered to pursue them? He had a
growing conviction that Drugget had not been after
the woman; he was after him. He had taken an
unnecessary risk by not heading straight back to
Little Fork after finding Belinda. He would need to
be a lot more careful in future. His thoughts turned
back to the cattle they had seen and as they did so, he
had a presentiment that there was a connection
between Cage Drugget and the Triangle S. If that was
the case, what was Schandler's role? Once he had
Belinda safely back in Little Fork, he would pay
another visit to the Triangle S, but he would do it his
own way. And he still hadn't solved the mystery of
what had happened to Applejack.

That same day had started like any other back in
Little Fork; a warm day with a soft breeze carrying the
scent of grass and flowers from the prairie. The town
was just stirring into life, and on the boardwalk
outside the general store young Melvin Lake was
sweeping away the dust and dirt. His lips were pursed

as he whistled a tuneless melody. He stopped and, leaning on his broom, stared away down Main Street where other enterprises were opening up or had already commenced the business of the day: Dalton's grocery store, the saddle shop, Morgan's Livery and Feed, the Old Bennington cafe. Just then the clock began to chime the hour and with a sigh Melvin took his broom and entered the dark interior of the store.

'Glad to see you doing a good job of sweeping,' the owner, Sam Tench, remarked. 'I guess that boardwalk must be the cleanest in town.'

Sam Tench's general store stocked all the main items anyone was likely to need and Melvin was to learn the whole business – buying, selling, stock-taking, keeping accounts – but since he had started, his time had been spent in more mundane activities. He liked meeting the customers and serving their needs, but even this grew dull by repetition.

'Quiet, isn't it?' Tench remarked. 'I guess it's early yet.'

Melvin busied himself setting out the stock, replenishing the shelves and checking to see what items were getting low. The first customer came in and was served by Tench. Then he retired to the stockroom and Melvin took over at the counter. More customers arrived. The growing day peered in through the store windows and a shaft of sunlight set motes of dust dancing in the air. Every now and then Melvin strode to the door of the shop and peered out. He looked up and down the street. Some horses were tied to the hitchrack outside the Blue Horse saloon. An old dog crossed the street to the board-walk he had just been cleaning and he bent down to stroke its head.

When the church clock struck twelve he checked with Tench that it was OK to take a break, and made his way to the Old Bennington cafe. Like the rest of the town, it was quiet, the only customer just leaving as Melvin came in.

'Hello Melvin,' Miss Myres began. 'What's it to be today? And don't worry, I haven't forgotten those doughnuts.'

Without waiting for a reply she shouted toward the kitchen:

'Hash up and make it quick!'

She knew from experience what Melvin wanted. Before the meal appeared, Miss Myres came to his table with a mug of steaming black coffee and a plate of doughnuts.

'They sure look good,' Melvin said.

'They are,' she confirmed. 'I had the recipe from my own ma and they don't come any better.'

'It's funny,' Melvin said, 'but I can hardly think of you as having a ma – or a pa for that matter.'

Miss Myres laughed.

'I'm not sure how to take that,' she replied. 'I suppose it's hard for a youngster like you to imagine, but I was young once too.'

Melvin could see that she was in a reflective frame of mind. He didn't object. He liked to hear her reminiscences.

'When I was a girl, we lived in a beautiful house

47

with arched windows and pillars like an old Greek temple at the entrance-way. It had a lovely lawn and flower beds and alongside it was a wonderful alley of horse chestnuts, beeches and maples.' She looked at him.

'You don't want to listen to an old lady's memories,' she said.

She stood up and moved to the kitchen, returning with a steaming mound of hash.

'Here you are,' she said, 'and there's more if you want it.'

Melvin began to eat. The food tasted glorious. He was hungry. He raised a fork to his mouth but it never got there. Suddenly the peace of the spring day was shattered into a million fragments by explosive sounds of shooting from the street. Someone outside was shouting, and instinctively Melvin leaped to his feet and ran to the door, closely followed by Miss Myres. In the street people were running. For no reason Melvin noticed that the horses, which had been fastened to the hitchrack were gone.

'The bank!' a voice shouted. 'Someone's robbing the bank!'

Melvin began to run towards the bank. It was not far. As he ran he observed a man on a horse just coming out of the alley which ran alongside the bank. He stopped and Melvin could see other horses behind him which he was holding on a rein. Coming to a halt, Melvin paused to draw breath.

Suddenly the doors of the bank flew open and two men ran out. They were carrying bags and wore bandannas pulled up over their faces. For an instant one of them paused to look at Melvin. At that moment another man came staggering out of the bank clutching at his shoulder from which blood was streaming. Melvin recognized him as Mr Grainger, the bank manager. Without, apparently, thinking of his own safety Mr Grainger ran up to the motionless gunman and grabbed at his face. The other gunman swung round and pumped two shots at close range into the bank manager's chest. Then he turned and, firing at Melvin, leaped on to one of the horses the man in the alley had been leading. Without further delay the three of them were galloping down the street, firing backwards as they went, but not before Melvin had had a clear view of the man who had paused to look at him. Even under the circumstances, he felt a stab of surprise. The face was that of an elderly man, with a white beard. Other people were running up now, including Baines, the deputy marshal. He was firing his Colt after the retreating bank robbers, but it was no use. They were clear of the town, leaving their dust hanging thickly in the air. The deputy marshal turned to Melvin.

'You OK boy?' he asked.

Melvin was quaking. The shock of the event had caught him and he could not stop shivering. Still he managed to tell the deputy that he was unhurt. Baines turned to the bank manager who lay bleeding in the dirt. Bending down he turned him over. He shook his head. A group of townsfolk had gathered.

'Someone get Doc Wilkins,' he said. Doc Wilkins

was also the town undertaker. No one needed to find him, however, for in the same instant he appeared in person.

'I'll take a look inside,' he said, and ran into the bank.

'Are you sure you'll be all right for a moment?' the deputy asked Melvin.

'Yeah, I'll be OK,' Melvin replied.

He was beginning to stop shaking but felt breathless and oddly weak. Following behind Doc Wilkins, Baines went inside the bank. There was a teller lying on the floor shot through his right leg. He was bleeding badly but the doctor seemed to think he would survive. Still feeling dazed, Melvin turned and began to walk back towards Miss Myres' Old Bennington cafe. As he approached he became dimly aware that a small group of townsfolk had gathered on the boardwalk nearby. Then he realized that a woman was screaming and a voice began to shout:

'Where's the doc! Get him here quick!'

Melvin turned, intending to go back to the bank, but some premonition made him move towards the group on the boardwalk instead. The crowd parted and he could see a figure lying there.

'No!' he cried. 'Not Miss Myres. Please not Miss Myres.'

She lay still, blood pumping from her mouth and throat. She had been shot in the neck. Melvin gagged and, turning his face, threw up over the dusty street. His knees gave way beneath him and he sank to the ground. He had been eating in Miss Myres' cafe only minutes before. She had been talking to him about her girlhood in Vermont. Tears were running down his cheeks and he was sobbing uncontrollably. He was only partially aware of what happened then. Feet came running. The deputy marshal was there and the doctor. They lifted him up and carried him into the cafe. His half-finished lunch and plate of doughnuts were standing on the table where he had left them. His coffee was still hot and a wisp of steam rose from it. The doctor produced a bottle and held it to his mouth. It contained whiskey and after it had burned its way down his throat he stopped sobbing and lay quietly. He became aware of somebody else being carried in and taken to a room at the back. He was conscious too of other people in the café – Sam Tench among them. There was a buzzing in his ears. Somebody was speaking to him, but he could not make out the words. From out in the street a horse neighed and people were shouting. It all became merged into one wall of sound and then things went black.

It was later that night when Marshal Cooley rode into town with Belinda Chesterton. Things had settled down but he sensed instinctively that something had happened in his absence. Lights were blazing in his office and as he rode by, the door flung open and Baines appeared on the veranda. His features expressed surprise at seeing Belinda but he quickly broke into a breathless explanation of what had happened in the marshal's absence.

'Whoa, slow down a bit,' Cooley said. 'Did anyone

get a good look at any of these *hombres*?'

'Young Melvin Lake got the best look at one of 'em.'

'Melvin's made a good recovery, you say?'

'Yeah. I went over to the house and he was able to give me a decent description. I got a Wanted dodger in preparation right now.'

The marshal was silent for a moment while he mulled over what his deputy had just told him. Baines continued to look at them both questioningly.

'This is Belinda Chesterton,' Cooley resumed. 'It's a long story. Wait here while I take her over to my place and see about the horse. I'll be back a soon as I can.'

'Sure thing, Rupe,' Baines replied.

The marshal spurred the tired horse and it moved forward.

'Is there a hotel?' Belinda said. 'I could register there.'

'You'll be better off stayin' with me and Selma,' Cooley replied.

'I don't want to put you to any further trouble.'

'Looks like we got a whole heap of it already. I don't think you stayin' over is likely to add to it.'

Belinda was silent for the few minutes it took to reach the marshal's house. Before they had alighted from the horse the door was opened and Selma appeared on the porch.

'I've got someone with me,' Cooley called.

Selma came down the path as they opened the gate. When she saw the girl her brain quickly registered the fact that she was stressed and tired.

'Come right on in,' she said. 'You look plumb tuckered.'

She put her arm around Belinda's shoulders, offering her support, and noticed the gash to her head.

'You poor dear,' she said. 'Let's get you safe indoors. I imagine you could do with something to eat? Once you're settled in, we'll see if you need the doctor.'

'I'll be fine,' Belinda said. 'Please don't put yourself out for me.'

'Nonsense,' Selma replied. 'What are folks for, if not to look out for one another?'

Cooley, coming up the path behind them, smiled to himself. He could always rely on his sister. It seemed like she and Belinda had already struck up an accord.

CHAPTER THREE

Long after the town had settled down for the night, Cooley sat up thinking about what had happened over the last couple of days and trying to make sense of it all. There were a number of questions that needed answers, and he felt that they were linked. The town had been quiet for a long time. It seemed too much to suppose that all the incidents that had taken place recently weren't connected. Why had Drugget attacked the wagon and killed Belinda's father? The answer to that one was probably quite simple: Drugget had a record of pointless violence; it was just the sort of thing he might be expected to do. But what was going on at the Triangle S? And now what about the bank robbery in Little Fork? Was Drugget behind that as well? Cooley felt guilty that he had not been present when the robbery took place. Innocent people had died while he had been out of town, ostensibly looking for Applejack. What had become of the oldster was another issue which remained unresolved. Searching for him might have been a valid reason for his absence, but he felt uncomfortable that so much of his time had been taken up with Belinda Chesterton. Although he had had little choice in the matter once he had discovered the wagon, he still felt that somehow he had allowed a private matter to come between himself and his civic duties. As he thought about the affair, he suddenly realized that there had been no horses with the wagon. Drugget must have taken them for his own purposes, but could there be something more significant about it? Had he reconstituted his gang and if so, how many gunslicks were involved? The thoughts and questions kept spinning round in his brain till finally he decided to try and call it a day. One way or another, he knew he would come up against Drugget at some stage. The man was out to destroy him; of that he had no doubt. The final question was whether he would come out of the confrontation alive, and solve the other problems in the process.

Next morning Cooley strolled over to the Lake house. He was greeted at the door by the older Mrs Lake, who ushered him into the living room. He glanced around. The room had a definite feminine feel apart from an old Kentucky rifle which hung on a rack above the fireplace. It had been Melvin's grandfather's gun and he had long admired it. It was a rifle-barrelled flintlock with elaborate brass fittings, and in its pips beneath the barrel was the ramrod. The patch box was a recessed brass-lidded compartment in the stock. As he was looking, Melvin's mother appeared in the kitchen doorway carrying a bowl on a tray.

'I'm sorry about this,' the marshal said.

'Marshal Cooley,' she replied. 'When I invited you to pay a visit, I sure didn't expect it to be on these terms.'

'How is young Melvin?' Cooley replied.

'Oh, he's fine. He's obviously upset about what happened to Miss Myres. We all are. I can hardly believe it myself.'

'I was out of town,' the marshal said. 'I should have been there.'

'Don't blame yourself. None of this was any of your doing.'

The older lady nodded in agreement.

'We've got Mr Cooley to thank for making this town a decent place to live in,' she said. 'I can remember when it wasn't always that way.'

'Would it be OK for me to have a word with Melvin?' the marshal said.

'Of course,' his mother replied. 'I was just going to give him this bowl of soup. Why don't you take it in?'

The marshal took the tray and advanced to the partly open door leading to Melvin's room. The boy was lying on his bed and looked up as Cooley entered.

'Hello, Mr Cooley,' he said.

'Hello,' the marshal replied. 'Here. Have some of this.'

It was Scotch broth with a crust of dry bread. Melvin sat up, propping his head with a pillow.

'What are you doing here?' he asked.

'I've come to see how you are. You've had a nasty shock.'

'I'm sorry,' Melvin said.

'Sorry about what?'

'Causing a fuss,' Melvin replied. 'I don't think I've handled things too well.'

'That's not true. You've been through a frightening experience. You don't need to make any apologies.'

Melvin raised the spoon to his mouth and drank. He dipped the bread into the broth and ate it. It seemed to make him feel better and the marshal suspected there was something in it.

'What about—?' he began, but the marshal cut him short.

'Miss Myres? I'm afraid she's dead.'

Melvin was silent. After a while the marshal spoke again.

'Do you feel able to answer a few questions?'

Melvin nodded.

'Are you sure?'

'Yes.'

The marshal hesitated, wondering how to begin.

'It's a nasty business,' he said.

'How is Mr Grainger?' Melvin asked.

Cooley shook his head.

'The bank teller will come through,' he said.

There was silence for a moment.

'Those robbers got way with a good deal of money,' he continued. 'My deputy's after them right now with a posse.'

He paused.

'I've got one witness who says he saw the leader with his bandanna down, but he couldn't give a description. He only had a brief glimpse and it was side-on.'

'I saw one of them,' Melvin said.

'Yes. So I understand. I figure chasin' this one up might take some time and I guess it'll be a county matter, but I don't intend letting them get away with it. Can you tell me what the man you saw looked like?'

Melvin had no difficulty remembering the gunslinger's features. They were etched on his brain and they were distinctive. He told this to the marshal who afterwards ran a finger across his brow and appeared to be deep in concentration.

'Tryin' to think if I've ever come across someone of that description before,' he said. 'What we'll do is get a written statement from you. Deputy Marshal Baines is already printing off a Wanted poster. You've done real good.'

He turned to go.

'I just want a word with your mother,' he said. 'Make sure you get back on your feet real soon. So long, for now.'

Melvin listened to his footsteps on the stairs. There was a pause and then he could hear the marshal talking to his mother and grandmother. Shortly afterwards the door slammed. As he walked away, the marshal was thinking hard. The boy's words had left him more puzzled than ever: the description he had given matched that of old Applejack.

Cage Drugget lay back in a big padded armchair and puffed on a fat cigar. He was feeling very pleased with himself. Since being released from jail, things had gone remarkably well. He had anticipated difficulties in resurrecting his old gang and taking over the Triangle S, but it had proved to be a simple matter. Like a ripe fruit, everything had fallen into his hands. There had been no overt opposition from Schandler; whatever his real feelings might be about the matter, there wasn't much he could do about it. Probably he remembered from the old days how ruthless Drugget had always been as leader of the gang. It was Drugget's money which had been behind the purchase of the Triangle S and it had been just bad luck that Rupe Cooley had succeeded in slapping him behind bars before he could take up residence.

It was fortunate, too, that a number of the old gang still worked on the ranch; when it came to a decision, they were wise enough to throw in their lot with their old leader. It might be wise sooner or later to eliminate Schandler and install Quinn as foreman, but first he would sound Schandler out on what could be done to improve the ranch other than by taking over some of the other ranches in the area. That much went without saying. As things stood, he could ride roughshod over the smaller ranches at roundup time, let his cattle roam at will on their overstocked ranges and apply extra pressure by a little cattle rustling. In addition, the ranch would provide good cover for his other activities. The bank robbery in Little Fork was just the start. That hadn't gone as smoothly as he would have liked. Next time he would take charge in person, when he didn't have to concern himself about other matters. That affair by the river had not gone the way he would have wanted either, but it was only a question of time till he caught up with Cooley. Maybe it was for the best that Cooley had succeeded in getting away on this occasion. When he finally caught up with him, he didn't want his revenge to be a quick affair. He wanted to savour it; he wanted to watch Cooley die slowly and painfully, and he knew a number of ways to make that happen.

It wasn't till after midnight that Cooley crossed the boundary between open range and Triangle S pasture. It suited his purposes that it was so dark. The moon was down and a scattering of stars appeared from time to time between scudding patches of cloud. The only sound was the creak of his harness and the soft thud of his horse's hoofs. Occasionally he caught a faint glimmer of light as it reflected from a cow's horn and the darkness was gathered into darker clumps where groups of cattle grazed. Directing his horse towards them, he slipped out of the saddle to check the brands. The first few were all Triangle S and he was beginning to think that his surmise about cattle rustling was wrong until he came across another group; when he examined them, he found that they bore Block T markings. He continued on his way. Most of the brands proved to be Triangle S but by the time he had completed his search had found not only Block T but also Wine Glass and Pig Pen brands. There weren't many of them, but enough to satisfy him that they had not simply strayed on to Triangle S property. There was little doubt in his mind that Schandler had been cattle rustling. What was more, he didn't seem to be making much effort to conceal the fact. Cooley had no great liking for Schandler, but he had been around for a long time and there had been no previous suggestion of cattle rustling. Sure, there had been a few isolated complaints recently about cattle going missing, but nothing definite. Did that mean something had happened to bring about this new situation? Again the marshal began to wonder whether there might be a connection between Schandler and Cage Drugget. He sat his horse, considering the matter for some time before coming to a decision. He would ride as far as the Triangle S ranch house and see if he could pick up any clues. If Cage Drugget had re-united with some of his old gang, there might be extra horses in the corral. He would just keep his senses alert for some indication of what might be taking place at the Triangle S.

He rode silently through the night till he saw the dark outline of the ranch buildings. He was approaching the place from the back so what he could see were the barns and stables. He brought his horse to a halt and, dropping from the saddle, proceeded to hobble it. Then he crept forward, keeping

61

low. He had been out to the ranch on various occasions so had a good idea as to its layout. The corrals were to his right. He didn't want to risk scaring the horses but he wanted to check their numbers. When he veered in their direction, his movement brought into view a side of the main ranch house and he was surprised to see a light in one of the windows. Maybe it wasn't so unusual, but at that time and in his heightened state of alertness it struck him as odd. He stopped and thought for a moment. It was a long shot, but it might be worth taking a peep.

Carefully, he stepped forward once more. The distance between him and the ranch house was further than it seemed. He skirted the barn and the corrals and slipped silently across the intervening space like a ghost. He reached the wall of the ranch house and flattened himself against it. Light spilled from the window and threw a patch of light across the dusty path. Drawing his gun, he crouched low and slithered forward till he was underneath the window frame. He could hear the muffled intermittent sound of voices but he couldn't make out what they were saying. Scarcely daring to breathe, he began to raise himself up till his eyes were just above the level of the window sill. Curtains were drawn across the window but through a slight gap at the side he was able to see part of the room. A man was sitting edgeways to him so that he could only see his profile. He couldn't be sure who else was there but he had the impression that there were more than two. He shifted his position slightly, taking immense care not to make sound, in order to try and see more and he was rewarded with a glimpse of a hand resting on a table. He strained his ears in an attempt to try and catch something of what they were saying, but it was no good. As he watched, the man's profiled head turned. It was only for a moment but it was enough for him to recognize the ugly features of Cage Drugget. He dropped below window level, waited for another few moments, and then carefully glanced through the gap in the curtain once more. Drugget's face was turned away but it was the hand on the table of which Cooley hoped to get a further view. The hand moved forward and he was able to see it better. Across the back of the hand he could discern the faded blue shape of a tattoo. He knew that shape – a snake's head – and he knew to whom the hand belonged: old Applejack. Taken together with the evidence of young Melvin Lake, there seemed no room for doubt. Unlikely as it seemed, old Applejack was riding with Cage Drugget and his gang. Another thought occurred to the marshal: it was probably Applejack who had revealed his whereabouts to the outlaw, leading to the shootout by the river.

Cooley waited a few moments longer before moving away from the window. Just as silently as he had come, he edged his way back along the wall of the ranch house. When he reached the corner he stopped to look about him but even if there had been somebody else on the prowl, the night was so dark they would probably have missed one another. After a few moments he crept into the open, making his way towards the corral and taking care to keep downwind of the horses. As he had surmised, there seemed to be more of them than he would have expected. There was no way of knowing just exactly what numbers Schandler was keeping, but it was another piece of circumstantial evidence. He was tempted to get inside the corral in order to check on some of the brands, but he didn't want to push his luck. It was unlikely that he would find anything of significance and he had the evidence he wanted of cattle rustling. It was a pity he had not been able to hear any of the conversation taking place inside the ranch house, but maybe it hadn't amounted to much. On the other hand, they were talking long into the night and it was only a day since the bank raid. Could they be plotting some other outrage? He glanced back. Light was still showing in the window. There wasn't much else he could do so he began to make his way back to where he had left the horse. By the time he had reached it and climbed into the saddle, the eastern horizon was showing the first indications of light.

Belinda Chesterton, waking from a fitful sleep and getting out of bed to take a window seat, watched Cooley ride up to the house. He dismounted and led the horse up the path to an out-building at the back which served as a stable. After what seemed a considerable time he reappeared and, opening the door silently, disappeared into the house. Suddenly she had a great desire to rush down the stairs and see him. More than that, for an inexplicable reason she had the need to feel his arms around her again. She began to sob and a tear ran down her cheek as she found herself thinking of her father. She recalled his lonely grave out on the prairie, a grave of which he would have been denied if it had not been for the marshal. Why were people so bad? Why had she and her father been attacked? It was only by pure luck that she had survived. They would have done a lot better after all to have stayed where they were. Their life hadn't been bad. Harpington now seemed a long way distant. She wasn't sure she had any desire to go there without her father, but what else was she to do?

It was late the next afternoon when the posse, led by Deputy Marshal Baines, arrived back in Little Fork. Cooley wasn't surprised to see them return.

'We lost their sign near where the trail bends towards the Triangle S spread,' Baines said.

'It took you a long while to get back.'

'We figured they might have taken to the hills so we rode on up into the high country but it was no good. Looks like they got clean away with the money.'

Baines poured himself a cup of coffee.

'How about you?' he said. 'You get a chance to speak to young Melvin Lake?'

'Yeah. What did you think about his description of the bank robber?'

Baines sat down and took a sip of the scalding black liquid.

'Can't say I've thought much about it,' he said.

'Seems like he weren't no tenderfoot though.'

'Yeah. Don't seem that way.'

Baines drank and looked at the marshal over the rim of his cup.

'Is there somethin' you ain't tellin'me?' he said.

The marshal had been thinking hard about Applejack for most of the day. He hadn't been able to make anything of what he had found out and wasn't sure what his next move should be. He had considered keeping his escapade of the previous night to himself but now saw no point in not taking his deputy into his confidence. He guessed it was just a misplaced reluctance to think the worst of the oldster. Wasting few words, he gave an account of what he had been doing. When he had finished, Baines let out a long whistle.

'Old Applejack,' he said. 'Are you sure . . . no, it can't be. There must be some kind of mistake.'

'I'd like to think so,' Cooley replied, 'but I can't see no other explanation.' The deputy shook his head.

'But how could Applejack have got mixed up with someone like Cage Drugget? It don't make any sense.'

Cooley got to his feet and poured a cup of coffee for himself, topping up Baines's at the same time.

'I guess there's only one way to find out,' Baines said, 'and that's to get on back to the Triangle S and put him under arrest.'

'Maybe,' Cooley replied. 'The only thing wrong with that is how I explain to Schandler that I knew

Applejack was at the ranch. And not just that. Right now I'm pretty sure where Drugget is. If we go ridin' in with all guns blazing—' he turned to Baines, 'figuratively speakin',' he said.

'I catch your drift,' the deputy replied.

'Well, if we do, we'll lose that little edge we got. If we're right about all this, we'll be puttin' Drugget and the rest of them on their guard. I'm wonderin' if it might not be better to play a different hand.'

'What you got in mind?'

'Sooner or later Drugget is goin' to show his cards. When he does, we'll be ready for him.'

'And what do you figure he's goin' to do?'

'I don't know. Could be another robbery. Maybe the overland stage. Maybe stirrin' up a range war, if all that cattle rustlin' is anythin' to go by. But I'm figurin' the thing to do might be to bide our time while we got Drugget bottled up where we know we can get him.'

The marshal finished, looking to his deputy for confirmation of his strategy.

'Ain't no good gonna come out of rushin' into things,' Baines replied. 'Let's see what happens.'

Cooley smiled. He didn't say anything about Cage Drugget having a personal vendetta against himself; nor that Drugget's most likely move would be against him.

'Guess I'll be gettin' on home,' Baines said.

'Yeah. You done a good job,' Cooley replied.

The deputy gave him a rueful look.

'Just wish we could have brought them varmints in

with us,' he said.

He walked out of the door and the marshal followed him shortly afterwards. Cooley started to walk in the direction of his house but suddenly felt a strange reluctance to go back. He couldn't understand why, but he felt awkward and he realized it was because of Belinda. But why should that be the case? He had got on perfectly well with her and she and his sister had struck up a friendship. He had told them when to expect him but although the clock had moved towards that time he felt himself hanging back. He was approaching an intersection when he stopped to reach in his pocket for his tobacco pouch. At the same moment a shot suddenly rang out and he felt the passage of a bullet. If he had continued walking he would have been hit. Someone screamed and he threw himself to the ground, drawing his six-gun in the same movement. He heard the sound of footsteps running down an alley that ran alongside the blacksmith's shop and was about to fire in that direction when he realized that there were people about and he couldn't take the risk. Instead, he got back to his feet and began to run in the direction of the alley.

It was dark in contrast to the broad street but he thought he saw a dim shape which disappeared round a corner. Keeping to the shadows, he hurled himself down the alley in pursuit. It was only a matter of seconds before he reached the end but when he peered around the angle of the last building he could see no sign of anybody. He looked up and down the narrow back street. There were a few run-down stores and a seedy saloon and then another alley leading towards a stretch of trees and some barns. He considered carrying the pursuit further but had a feeling it would prove fruitless. Instead he decided to retrace his footsteps and check that things were OK back there. He remembered the scream and when he turned into the main street he saw a woman clutching a stanchion, her other hand held to her chest.

'Are you OK, ma'am?' he said.

She looked up at him and nodded. She seemed slightly breathless.

'Can I accompany you to where you were going?' he said.

A slight smile appeared at the corners of her mouth.

'No, I'll be fine, Marshal,' she replied.

A couple of other people joined them.

'I don't want to make a fuss,' she said.

The marshal looked at the newcomers.

'Someone took a shot,' he said. 'He probably had too much to drink at the Blue Horse. I don't suppose either of you saw anything?'

They shook their heads.

'Well, looks like the excitement is over,' he said.

A little group of spectators had gathered and Cooley waited till they had gone about their business once more before he turned and made his way back to the alley. He bent down, looking for boot marks in the dust. There were some, but he could deduce nothing of any significance from them. He looked about for the cartridge case and eventually located it. He held it up to the light. He guessed it was from a .44 calibre Colt Frontier Cavalry model; there was nothing distinctive about that either. Slipping it into his shirt pocket, he turned back and continued his interrupted way down the main street. His first thought was that Drugget had taken a shot at him, but as he considered the matter further, he became convinced that someone else was involved. Drugget would want to savour his revenge; he wouldn't have gone about it in this cack-handed way. He had no need to skulk down back-alleys. But who else would want him dead? His thoughts turned to old Applejack. Could it be him? He had known the oldster a long time and it didn't seem credible that he would commit such an act. On the other hand, there was that description of him given by young Melvin Lake and the evidence of his own eyes the previous night. But even so, what could the oldster have against him personally? Surely he was beginning to credit Applejack with an unnecessary catalogue of crimes. His thoughts went back to the afternoon he had seen Applejack ride into town on the burro. At the time he had had no reason to question what the oldster said about finding gold. He had seen some of the gold dust. Of course, in the light of what had happened since, that meant nothing. It could have been iron pyrites. The oldster had said he had found it on the Indian River above the oxbow lake. Now he thought about it, Applejack had been fairly free in his account. He had even warned him about shooting his mouth off in the Blue Horse saloon. At the time he had been concerned about the oldster's safety, but could there have been some other significance in Applejack's words? Come to that, was it likely that he would have found gold in the vicinity of the oxbow lake? The land was pretty flat and the river flowed slowly – that was how the oxbow lake got formed in the first place. It needed some consideration, but already he was beginning to think it might be a good idea to take a ride out that way. The problem was that he already felt guilty about having been out of town when the robbery took place. He didn't like to absent himself again, especially as it would take a few days to get there and back. Preoccupied by his thoughts, he realized that he was almost at his house. The lamp shining in the parlour window looked cosy and inviting and, contrary to his previous feelings, he found he was excited about the prospect of seeing Belinda again.

Dusk had fallen now, and at first his eyes did not realize that the figure approaching him down the path was that of Belinda herself. Then, as she opened the gate and came out to meet him, he saw her and stopped in his tracks. She had put on a blue dress with a high white collar and her hair hung loosely to her shoulders. She looked more beautiful than he had remembered.

'Hello, Mr Cooley,' she said. 'Selma and I have started supper, but it's a lovely evening and I thought a little stroll might help to build up both our appetites.'

'Sounds like a good idea to me,' he replied.

Unconsciously and without any sign of awkwardness, she took his arm. They walked past the house and carried on a little way till, taking a turn, they came to the little wooden bridge which crossed a stream.

'If you follow this,' Cooley said, 'eventually you come to a branch of the Indian River. It's quite a long walk but it's real nice.'

'Let's stop here for a moment,' she said.

They stood on the bridge and watched the water as it purled beneath them.

'Your sister is very nice,' Belinda said.

'Yeah. She was teachin' for a while in Harpington, but she came back. It seemed convenient for us to live together.'

'Harpington? That's where we were bound, my father and I.'

She looked down into the water.

'I'm sorry,' Cooley said. 'I should have realized. . . .'

She turned to him with the suggestion of a smile on her face which made it even more appealing.

'It's all right,' she said.

'Come on, why don't we walk a little further?' he replied.

'Yes, but we mustn't go too far. Remember that supper is almost ready.'

This time she did not take his arm and he felt surprisingly disappointed. They carried on strolling side by side. He wanted to ask what her plans were now. Did she still intend carrying on to Harpington? He guessed that she would do so, but the thought of it didn't please him. But what else was she to do? He felt sensitive about broaching the subject. For the moment he was happy just to be with her. It was a feeling he hadn't experienced before.

'By the way,' she said after a few moments, 'did you ever find out what happened to your friend Applejack? That was his name, wasn't it?'

The question came as a surprise. He realized that for the brief time he had been with Belinda, he had forgotten all about the oldster and everything else connected with Cage Drugget.

'No, not yet,' he said.

'Well, I hope you find him soon. I've got Applejack to thank for you rescuing me, remember. If you hadn't been searching for him, you wouldn't have found me.'

Her words were glib enough but somehow, to Cooley they seemed to carry an additional significance. He laughed softly.

'I hadn't looked at it that way,' he said. 'I guess you're right. That's somethin' I got to thank the old devil for.'

They paused and looked at each other. He felt a sudden awkwardness.

'Come on,' Belinda said. 'I think we'd better be getting back. Your sister will be expecting us.'

The next morning Cooley was in his office early. While he waited for Baines to arrive there was a knock on the door. When he answered it, he was surprised to see young Melvin Lake standing there.

'Melvin!' he said. 'Come on in.'

The youngster shuffled inside.

'I didn't expect to see you. How are you feelin'?'

'I'm fine now,' Melvin said. 'In fact, I'm starting back to work at Mr Tench's store. I'm on my way there now.'

'That's good. How do you like workin' for Mr Tench?'

'It's OK,' the boy answered, 'but it ain't what I want.'

'What is it you want?'

Melvin looked slightly sheepish. 'I'd like to be a lawman like you.'

Cooley gave a laugh and then, realizing that the boy might misinterpret it, broke it off short.

'Well,' he said, 'it's a fine thing to have a respect for the law, but the job isn't everything you might imagine it to be.'

'You ain't stuck behind a counter all day long. You're doin' something useful.'

'And you think that Mr Tench and the rest of the folks around here aren't doin' just that? Believe me, it's the likes of Mr Tench who make things work. The ordinary folk, they're the ones who'll build this country.'

'But you get to do somethin' different every day.'

'Don't you believe it, son. I spend a lot of time just

sittin' and waitin'. I got paperwork to do. Most of the time nothin' happens. That's a good thing. That's the way it should be. A quiet town is a good town. The less I have to do, the better things are.'

'That's what my father used to say. He told me this country is changing. It might be slow, he said, it might take time, but it's changing. It's growing and I want you to grow with it.'

'He was right, son.'

'I never used to understand what he was driving at. Once he took down that rifle from the wall—'

'The old Kentucky rifle?'

'Yes. He told me that it belonged to my grandfather, that in its day it was the best. He said that with guns like it men fought the wilderness and made their way west, through the Appalachians into Pennsylvania and Kentucky. But he said it was obsolete, and so were the people who used it. The mountain men, the pioneers, they were the trailblazers and the guides, but it was the settlers who built the land.'

'Isn't that just what I been sayin'?' the marshal interposed. 'And I tell you what: the future will be different; it will need people with different skills, people who can build things that last, who can establish businesses that will create wealth and security.'

The boy looked unconvinced.

'You'll see what we both mean one day,' the marshal said.

He had sudden idea.

'If being a storekeeper don't appeal to you, how

about becomin' a lawyer? You don't have to carry a gun to represent the law.'

Melvin's eyes flickered.

'Say, I never thought of that.'

'The country is goin' to require lawyers, men that can apply the rules and principles we've all fought to establish. It's somethin' to think about. And I'm willin' to bet your father would be right proud of you if you qualified.'

The boy looked quite animated.

'Thanks, Mr Cooley,' he said. 'I've enjoyed talkin' to you.'

He moved towards the door.

'Is that all you came about?' the marshal said.

Melvin stopped and turned.

'By Jiminy,' he said. 'I almost forgot. When I told my mother about that man whose face I saw, she said it sounded familiar. I guess she must have thought about it overnight, because this morning she said she thought she knew who it might be. She said it sounded like a description of a man called Applejack. She said to tell you.'

The marshal nodded.

'Thanks for that, Melvin,' he replied. 'I appreciate you making the effort.'

'Do you know him?'

'I know a man called Applejack. I don't know whether he was the one involved in the robbery.'

'It's Miss Myres' funeral tomorrow,' Melvin said. 'I hope you catch them all.'

'Leave it to me,' Cooley replied. 'I won't let them

get away with it.'

When the boy had gone he went to the stove and put some coffee on to boil. By the time it had brewed the door opened again and Baines entered.

'That sure smells good,' he said.

Cooley poured him a cup. He had been intending discussing the whole situation with his deputy but something now made him anxious to get on his way towards the ox-bow lake. He still felt a slight degree of unease about leaving Baines behind, but he felt surer of what he needed to do. As they drank, he kept his explanations and his plans to a minimum. When he mentioned Applejack the deputy sat up.

'It's funny,' he said. 'I don't know the man like you do, but I been thinking about what Melvin Lake told me, and it seemed the description he gave sounded a bit like the oldster.'

'Could match a lot of old timers. Could have even been a disguise.'

The deputy grunted.

'I just about got that Wanted poster ready,' he said. 'Either way, it should help.'

'You OK about handlin' things back here again?'

'That's my job,' Baines said.

He glanced at Cooley's shirt.

'Since you don't know just what you could be ridin' into,' he advised, 'it might be an idea to keep that badge out of sight.'

Later that morning, Cooley set off for the Indian River.

It was a good ride and he allowed the horse to set

its own pace. After a time he could see the outline of the hills away to his left. That was where Baines had led the posse but his own route led him towards the low-lying country by the river. At times he was close to the water; at other times its meandering course led it away from him. The banks were lined with tall cypress trees and occasionally an eagle flew overhead. That night he camped quite close to the water and next day had his first view of the lake, shimmering in the bright sun. He continued riding till he had left the oxbow some distance behind. The ground was flat and swampy but, seeing a slight incline ahead of him, he rode to it. Before reaching the top he halted, slid from the saddle, and, after tethering his horse, moved cautiously to the crest of the rise from where he had a view over the country. Away off to his left he was surprised to see what looked like several low shacks. One building was considerably larger than the others and outside, by the door, stood a tin wash basin and a pail of water; from the eaves of the hut hung a soiled piece of material which, he guessed, acted as a towel. The indications were that the place was not deserted. He looked for horses, but could not see any. Either the residents were away for the moment or the horses were in the stables. He looked upwards and saw a group of horsemen coming into view. Flattening himself against the ground, he watched closely. There were six of them, and, as the horsemen approached the shacks, a figure emerged to meet them, joined by another from one of the smaller huts, which he guessed was probably used as a stables.

The first horseman dismounted and said something to the man who had emerged from the barn. The others followed suit. The men were talking and gesticulating, then the one who had come out of the buildings took charge of the horses while the others went inside. Cooley wasn't sure what to do next. Who would be using the buildings? There would be a considerable degree of risk involved in getting closer. The ground between him and the huts was pretty well bare of cover and he imagined the men inside would be watchful. Still, he had almost made up his mind to give it a try when his meditations were interrupted by the sound of a rifle being levered behind him.

'Don't move a muscle!' a voice hissed.

He felt the point of a gun in the small of his back.

'Make one false move and you're dead.'

Cooley was still lying flat on the ground. There was nothing he could do as the man removed his guns and flung them to one side. He cursed himself for having let his guard drop. He had been distracted by the arrival of the riders but he should have known better.

'Now, get up real slow and careful.'

Cooley did as he was told and gently raised himself from the ground.

'Don't bother to turn around,' the man ordered. 'Put your hands above your head and start walking. And remember, I've got a mighty nervous trigger finger.' Cooley began to walk across the open ground

between him and the buildings. He would have liked
to look round to see the man behind him, but realized that all he could do for the present was obey his
commands. They were more than halfway towards
the huts. Cooley watched for any signs of activity
ahead of him. He reckoned the men inside must
have seen the two of them approaching by now, but
no one appeared. When they had gone a few more
strides the man behind him called in a loud voice:

'Quinn, boys, I got me a snooper! I'm bringin'
him in!'

A few moments later the door opened and two
men emerged. Cooley gasped inwardly. One of them
was old Applejack! As Cooley approached, the
oldster stepped forward.

'Ray,' he said. 'Ray Streeter!'

The other man turned to him.

'You recognize this *hombre*?' he said.

'Sure do, Quinn,' the oldster confirmed.
'Leastways, I think I do. He used to ride with us.
Before your time it would be, but some of the boys
might remember him.'

Quinn looked closely at the marshal before
addressing the man who had brought Cooley in.

'Good work,' he said. 'You can put your gun down
now. Leave him to me.'

'OK boss,' the man grunted.

'Take a look up yonder and see if you can find his
horse. Leave it behind the stables and then join us.'

He turned to Cooley.

'I don't know what this is all about,' he said, 'but

I'm going to find out. You'd better have a good story. We none of us take to strangers nosin' around.'

He turned to lead the way inside the building. There was not much furniture; just a table and a few broken-down chairs, a couple of three-legged stools and some bunks on which the other men Cooley had seen riding in were lying. The fireplace gave evidence of usage but there was no stove. The ground was packed hard, and the windows were empty of glass. All this Cooley's eyes took in as he was ushered to one of the rickety chairs and ordered to sit down.

'Start talkin',' Quinn snapped.

'Name's Streeter,' he said. 'Ray Streeter.'

'Just like I said,' Applejack added.

'Shut up,' Quinn retorted.

'He rode with Prentice in the old days,' the oldster replied, ignoring Quinn's command. 'He was one of the boys pulled the Clear Creek bank job.'

'That right?' Quinn barked.

'Yeah,' Cooley replied.

'So what happened?'

Cooley was having to think quickly.

'After the Clear Creek job I pulled out – had a sudden hankerin' to sniff Gulf breeze. Did me some brush poppin', bronco-bustin'. Figured I could steal a start by doing a bit of maverickin' on my own account. Didn't get nowhere. Not much to tell. Figured in the end I could do better hittin' the owlhoot trail again. So here I am.'

'I don't believe you,' Quinn said.

'Too bad. I got information could be real useful to

you boys. But I want to be counted in.'

'Personally I see no reason not to shoot you right now.'

'He could be right, Quinn,' one of the men remarked.

'We might get stretched,' someone else said. 'Might be worth havin' him along.'

Quinn thought for a moment.

'Go on,' he said to Cooley. 'What information have you got that could interest me?'

'I know where the rest of that Clear Creek loot is stashed, and there's enough to make you boys rich.'

'And what do you get out of this?'

'I got a score to settle. I can't do it on my own.'

It seemed to Cooley that his story was pretty thin, but he was having to think on his feet and at least he might buy some time. Quinn stroked his chin.

'We'll talk about this later,' he said with a grimace.

He gestured to a couple of the men.

'Put him in the outhouse. I don't trust him. One of you stand guard.'

Cooley got to his feet. As he crossed the yard, he saw his horse being led into a meadow behind the building he guessed was being used as a stable, by a tall man with drooping mustachios. Again he uttered a curse for allowing himself to get into this mess. He couldn't imagine what Applejack was doing here, but by acting on the oldster's prompt he had succeeded in gaining time. He needed to think of a way out – and quick.

CHAPTER FOUR

There was an atmosphere of expectancy hanging over the Triangle S. Drugget's men had been growing a little restless. Most of them were not accustomed to ranch work and they left the regular running of the spread to Schandler's cowhands. They had been looking for action and it seemed it was in the offing. Cage Drugget had sent word that everyone was to be available in the next couple of days and riders had been despatched to bring in his gunslicks from the surrounding territory. He sat at a table in the living room of the ranch house looking at a map when there was a knock on the door and Schandler appeared.

'You wanted me?' he asked.

Drugget cast a cold eye on him. There were few people in whom he ever placed any trust and Schandler wasn't one of them.

'Yes,' he said. 'I want you to ride into Little Fork and take a look around. Call in at the marshal's office. Make nice with him.'

'Make nice with him? Why would I do that?'

Drugget breathed heavily.

'Use your brains, if you got any. After that bank job it won't hurt just to lull him into a false sense of security. Kinda show him the Triangle S is on the side of the law.'

'You think he's got suspicions?'

'No, I don't think that. But like I say, it don't do any harm to keep him sweet.'

Schandler had a feeling that he had already, perhaps, pushed things too far.

'Sure,' he said. 'I see what you mean. I'll get saddled up and leave right away.'

He turned on his heels and walked through the door. Drugget watched him till he was gone and then he turned back to the outspread map.

Cooley opened his eyes. It was dark in the outhouse and he could see nothing. He sensed that it was still night but there was a feeling of dawn in the air. He was thirsty and hungry. He had not eaten or drunk since setting off the day before. Nobody had come since he had been locked in. He had spent time trying to think of a way out, but there was none. The outhouse was quite well constructed and there was only a small barred opening high in the wall. There was nothing in it but a bucket he had used to relieve himself. It seemed to him that his best plan would be to wait on events and continue to try and string Quinn along. Whatever Applejack's role was, it seemed he had intervened to save his life. Maybe he could do something more to get him out of this jam?

He sat with his back against the wall facing the door. Soon his ears detected a few early noises – a bird calling, the snicker of a horse. Some light began to filter through the window. Then after a time he heard voices. He guessed it was someone talking to the guard outside. There was a sound of muffled laughter. He listened closely but could not make out any of the conversation. The footsteps faded. There was something about that laugh that disturbed him. He began to think again about his story, and the more he went over it the thinner it seemed. Why had they left him in here all this time? Maybe his original notion was wrong; maybe he needed to seize the initiative. He couldn't just count on Applejack coming up with something. But what was he to do? If only he had his guns. What could he use as a weapon? His eyes fell on the bucket and the glimmer of a plan began to emerge.

He focused his attention on trying to visualize the layout of the place. It was his custom to observe his surroundings closely, and he had a pretty clear picture of the set-up. If he could make it to the stable he might have a chance. Better still, if there was a horse tied to the hitchrail. He calculated the distance between himself, the stable and the main building. If he could get quickly out of the door, the corner of the outhouse would cut him off from view. He would have to come out in the open again, but then it was only a few yards to the shelter of the stable. Maybe someone would be inside. There was no way of knowing. The moment when the outhouse door opened would be crucial. He would be standing behind it and as soon as the gap was wide enough, he would dash the slop-bucket into the face of the first man and hope to grab his gun. Then he would run for the stable. It wasn't much of a plan; a lot would depend on wrestling that gun away from the guard and on how many of them there might be.

Taking hold of the bucket, he waited by the door. Time passed. He began to go over it all again; perhaps he had been right the first time. Maybe his best chance lay in just trying to string along the outlaws while keeping on the alert for the main chance. Then he heard the sound of voices and further thought ceased. There was a scuffing of boots on the packed earth of the yard. The footsteps drew closer. Damn, there seemed to be a number of them. The footfalls stopped; there was more conversation. Straining his ears, he could just about distinguish individual sounds. He thought he heard a reference to the barn, the word 'beam'. Then the footsteps resumed. Some of them seemed to be taking a different direction. Others were getting very close and then, sharp as a rifle crack, he heard the mocking voice of Quinn call out:

'Fasten it good, boys!'

The sudden realization flashed across his brain: they were going to hang him! He had no choice now. There was a sound of keys being juggled in the lock. The door started to swing open. A wedge of light began to disperse the dark shadows as Cooley sprang forward, swinging the bucket and smashing it into the face of the person behind the door. Over he went and caught by surprise, their eyes unaccustomed to the blackness within, the others reeled backwards. There were two of them. Quinn shouted a curse as the contents of the bucket flew into his face. One of the men had dropped his rifle and Cooley caught it up as, with one move, he began sprinting round the corner of the outhouse towards the stable building.

From the direction of the barn a figure emerged and began firing, but he too was startled and it was still gloomy in the yard. From somewhere a cock crowed. Hurtling forward, Cooley flung himself through the stable door. Inside, the horses were restive as more shots began to thud into the outer wall. Cooley carried on running. Further down was a kind of runway which led outside the back of the barn to a meadow where, to his surprise, he saw his own big roan hobbled. In an instant he had it loose and was swinging up on to its back. There was no chance to saddle it, but he had ridden bareback plenty of times before. Digging his heels into its flanks, he urged it forwards as the first of his pursuers emerged around the side of the stables. Raising the rifle with one hand, Cooley let go a shot which took the man in the shoulder and sent him spinning. The man's own gun exploded and the roan reared up, almost throwing Cooley from its back. The situation was not looking good as two more gunslicks emerged to block his way. He was trying to bring the horse back under control so could not bring the rifle round to a firing position. A shot rang out and a bullet passed over his head. Still trying to calm the horse, he became aware of a figure which had appeared as if from nowhere. Despite all the distractions, he recognized Applejack. As one of the men advanced on Cooley, the oldster's rifle spat lead and the man fell backwards. The second man turned his attention to the newcomer and Applejack's rifle spoke again; the gunnie fell to the ground almost under the hoofs of Cooley's horse. With a last desperate effort and despite the lack of harness, he succeeded in getting the roan under control. The horse leaped forwards. Cooley was away now, with no chance to thank the oldster for coming to his assistance. Once again Applejack had retrieved the situation. He heard the crump of shots and a singing of lead as the horse galloped across the open meadow and leaped a low, broken-down fence beyond. The roan was fresh and Cooley soon put distance between himself and the huts.

'Good boy!' he shouted.

The wind caught his words and sent them flying backwards. He had a start on Quinn's men and was gaining confidence with every stride of the horse when he saw a couple of riders coming from his right. He urged the horse away from them as they engaged in pursuit. Rifle shots cracked but he wasn't too bothered. He had a decent start on them and it wasn't easy taking aim from a running horse at a moving target. They were running level and the chase seemed to have been going on a considerable time when suddenly his horse stumbled and he was thrown to the side, landing with a heavy thud beside the fallen animal. He had hurt his shoulder but rolled quickly to lie alongside the animal's back. Using it as cover, he raised his rifle, and as his two pursuers came on, fired one shot and then a second. The first caused the nearest rider's horse to rear up, toppling him from the saddle. The second hit the gunman full in the chest and he slid backwards, being dragged behind as his right foot remained stuck in the stirrup. Cooley turned his attention to the first rider. He must have discarded his rifle because he began firing his six-gun. He was stretched on the ground, making a difficult target. As the shots from his revolver tore up the ground nearby, Cooley took careful aim with his rifle and squeezed the trigger. The man jumped and jerked and then lay still.

Slowly and carefully Cooley rose to his feet. It did not take long for him to satisfy himself that both men were dead. The rider whose foot had been caught had been dragged by his horse a fair distance and was a mangled mess of blood, bone and tissue. Cooley took his guns and ammunition and then walked back to examine his own horse. It had struggled to its feet and did not appear to be badly hurt. He guessed it had caught its hoof in a gopher hole. Taking the other man's saddle, he soon had the roan harnessed. At least for the moment there were no signs of further pursuit. Either the gunslicks had lost him or, for whatever reason, they had at least temporarily given up the chase. He swung into leather.

His first instinct was to head in the direction of the oxbow lake but that would mean going back towards Quinn. As he was weighing up the situation he saw another rider in the distance. He sat his horse for a few moments and was just about to apply his spurs when something about the newcomer stopped him. The man was coming towards him at speed and was making no attempt to conceal his progress. He drew the rifle from the scabbard where he had replaced it and raised it in readiness. The man was getting closer and suddenly began to wave his arms. What was he doing? Suddenly the realization dawned that the rider was Applejack.

'What in tarnation?' he said to the roan.

Still holding the rifle in readiness, he began to move towards the approaching rider and in another few moments the oldster brought his horse to a halt in a cloud of dust.

'Cooley!' he said. 'Quick, let's get way out of here.'

Cooley opened his mouth to reply but the oldster was already off again. Replacing the rifle in its sheath, Cooley set off in pursuit. The two of them continued riding hard but presently the oldster's speed dropped and they continued at a steadier pace. They were approaching some rougher country that was known as the Indian Breaks. There were outcroppings of rocks and scarred bluffs cut by dry watercourses. The oldster seemed to know his way and avoided the more difficult sections of the terrain, Cooley taking care to follow closely in his wake. They carried on a little further till the oldster dropped down into an arroyo where he finally drew to a halt. Cooley rode up alongside. The oldster looked at him and Cooley had the distinct impression that there was a twinkle of amusement in his eyes.

'Applejack, you old coyote,' he said. 'Whatever in hell is this all about? I reckon I deserve an explanation!'

It didn't take long for Cooley and the oldster to make themselves comfortable. Once they had built a fire and eaten, they settled down to drink coffee and smoke.

'Well,' Cooley began, 'I reckon I owe you for comin' to my help. I sure appreciate it. But I think it's about time you told me just what's goin' on.'

The oldster took a long sip of the black coffee.

'Guess so,' he said.

His words were followed by a period of silence.

'Go on then,' Cooley snapped.

'Give me another moment,' the oldster said. 'I'm gettin' so I can't exactly remember just how things happened.'

'How about if I prompt you then. That claim you staked, does it really exist?' The oldster shook his head.

'Nope,' he said. 'That yarn was to throw Baines off the scent.'

'Baines?'

'Yeah, the deputy marshal. I wasn't sure if he could be trusted. I wanted to kinda give you a clue without bein' too obvious. I figured you'd be talkin' with Baines.'

'I don't get this at all. What's Baines got to do with it? And what could he not be trusted with?'

The oldster cleared his throat and spat into the fire.

'Let me ask you one thing,' he said. 'After that bank robbery in Little Fork, did you send Baines off in charge of the posse?'

'Sure,' Cooley replied.

'And did the posse catch up with the robbers?'

'No. But I don't see how that signifies anythin'.'

'Maybe it doesn't. On the other hand, maybe I was right to be cautious.'

Cooley had a sudden inclination to seize the oldster by his shirt collar.

'You're not makin' this any clearer,' he said.

The oldster took another drink of coffee and began to splutter.

'Hell, that went down the wrong way,' he said.

'I'll do the chokin' soon,' Cooley responded.

'OK,' Applejack replied. 'I know I ain't doin' much of a job of this so let me throw in a few facts and try to keep it simple. In the first place, I'm workin' for Wells Fargo. I'm workin' for myself as well but that's a different matter. Fact is, I once rode with Cage Drugget's outfit. That was way back before you caught up with him and put him behind bars. I ain't proud of some of the things I did in those days but sometimes a man gets down on his luck and finds himself in situations he don't know how.'

'No need to explain,' Cooley said. 'Those days are gone.'

'Yeah. Trouble is, they weren't gone. I thought they were till I heard Drugget was out of jail and then they just come back and hit me in the face. You see, thanks to my involvement with Drugget I lost my wife and my home and everythin' I had.'

'Sorry to hear of it,' Cooley said. 'I never figured you were ever married.'

'Was once. I don't need to go into details. She tried to make me see the error of my ways gettin' caught up with Drugget and his gang but it seemed like easy money and I was naive enough to think that it could all happen without anybody bein' hurt. Hurt bad, that is. It was partly because of the way I felt about Liza that I carried on. I wanted to get her nice things and make her life easy. All the time she was tryin' to tell me that was not what she wanted. In the end I lost her. She couldn't take it no more.'

He paused and Cooley didn't interrupt. Presently the oldster leaned forward to refill his mug.

'When I heard Drugget was out of jail and formin' a new gang, I decided to renew acquaintance. I figured he was bound to be plannin' on doin' some-thin' real bad and I decided I'd be right there on the inside.'

'Where does Wells Fargo come into it?'

'They're owed a heap of money by Drugget. They were never able to pin him down, but they know he was responsible for a whole lot of stagecoach rob-beries. You know what they say: "Wells Fargo never forgets". You could say I'm kind of an unofficial agent.'

'They contacted you?' Cooley said.

'I contacted them. I already got plenty on Drugget's recent activities that might interest them, but the big one is right down the line.'

Cooley thought for a moment.

'Is that what you were plannin' the other night?' he said.

The oldster looked startled.

'I was out at the Triangle S. I saw you through the window. Leastways, I saw your hand.'

Involuntarily, Applejack glanced down at the back of his hand.

'Nobody else I know got a snake like that adornin' his flesh,' Cooley said.

The oldster laughed.

'You know somethin' about all this already,' he said.

'Figure so. Am I right in thinkin' Drugget has taken over the Triangle S?'

'Yeah, you are. It was always his. Schandler was just there to take care of it, temporary like.'

'And Drugget's usin' it as his base of operations?'

'Yup, but it's more than that. Once he's carried out his final job, he figures to stay there, take over most of the surrounding ranches, and who knows? Maybe run for senator some day.'

'Has he been rustlin' cattle?'

'Sure. And that bank job was carried out by some of his boys.'

'What about an attack on a man and his daughter ridin' a wagon?' Cooley said, looking closely at the oldster's face as he said it. He was sure that no flicker of knowledge crossed Applejack's features.

'Don't know nothin' about that,' he said.

'Never mind,' Cooley said. 'You were sayin' somethin' about a final job Drugget's got planned?'

'Yeah. This is the crux of the matter. Trouble is, I might have blown it now.'

'Why is that?'

'Drugget was gettin' suspicious of me anyway, but now I've spun that line about you once ridin' the owlhoot trail and made myself absent by comin' out here, he ain't gonna be fooled any longer. I don't think I can afford to go back.'

'I can see that,' Cooley said. 'And I sure appreciate you comin' to my rescue. Things were lookin' pretty bad for me till you intervened.'

'You were pretty quick on the uptake. I liked that yarn about knowin' where the Clear Creek loot is stashed.'

He glanced at the marshal.

'Say, that weren't true, were it?'

It was Cooley's turn to laugh.

'Didn't you make that one up?' he replied.

The oldster grinned. He drew a little closer to the fire.

'So what's Drugget got planned?' Cooley continued.

'It's a big bank robbery. Least I think so. That affair in Little Fork was just a practice run.'

'A practice run which got two people killed,' Cooley replied.

'Yeah. Quinn was in charge of that operation. That's why he's hidin' out up here.'

'What is that place?' Cooley said.

'It's a few shacks that were left behind by some trappers that used to work on the Indian River system. I make use of them sometimes myself. Showing it to Drugget was one of my contributions to the gang. It should have been possible for the posse to track Quinn this far.'

'You statin' your suspicions about Baines again?' Cooley said. 'So far as I've had dealin's with him, he's a good man. I trust him. What reasons you got not to?' The oldster shrugged.

'Drugget's got supporters in town. It's been his way in the past. In the long term, he's aimin' to gain control of Little Fork as well as the Triangle S.' The marshal was thoughtful.

'What's stoppin' me from goin' back to Little Fork, roundin' up a posse, and ridin' right back here myself to arrest Quinn?'

'Because you ain't got nothin' on him. Or on Drugget yet, come to that.'

The marshal glanced at Applejack.

'In fact, the only evidence I got is against you,' he said.

If he expected the oldster to be taken aback, he was mistaken.

'You mean the boy?' he asked.

'Yes. He gave me a pretty good description. Did you have to be actually takin' part in the robbery?'

'I didn't have much choice. You got to believe me,

I did my best to keep things from gettin' out of hand.'

'You didn't do a very good job,' the marshal replied.

'I feel real bad the way things turned out. Even Drugget thought it was a botched job. That was what we were discussin' the night you saw us through the window. I was hopin' I might find out more about the big operation, but it didn't come up.'

'What do you know?'

'Only that I think it's gonna be another bank job, but much bigger than the Little Fork caper. And it's comin' off real soon.'

Cooley finished his cigarette and flicked the butt into the fire.

'There ain't too many towns around here,' he said. 'It should be possible to work out where it's gonna be. Maybe some place that's taking a big deposit of money.'

'I don't know. That's the problem.'

They lapsed into silence. The fire burned down and Applejack threw some brush on to it. They rolled another cigarette and poured more coffee. Cooley's head was filled with thoughts about what had happened and what to do next. Apart from every other issue, one other thing puzzled him. Who had taken that pot-shot at him? Whoever it was hadn't been very competent so he guessed it was not one of Drugget's gunslicks. He considered what Applejack had said about his deputy. Could it have been him? He still couldn't give credence to the oldster's suspicions and besides, the same argument against it being one of Drugget's gunslicks was equally applicable. If Baines had wanted to shoot him, he wouldn't have missed. He recalled the incident. He had been talking with Baines and then the deputy had left not long before Cooley. He could easily have taken up a position in the alley. Baines used a Frontier Cavalry, the weapon Cooley thought the bushwhacker had used, but that didn't mean anything; plenty of people carried that model. Baines had been away with the posse and had not got back till late in the afternoon. What had he been doing all that time? Who else had been in that posse? Thinking hard, he remembered that Baines had said that they had ridden up into the high country, but Quinn and the rest of the bank robbers had made for the oxbow lake. No, this line of thinking was crazy. He had appointed Baines as deputy marshal himself and he trusted him. It was not long before that he had been suspecting old Applejack of firing the shot. Suddenly his thoughts were broken into by the oldster's voice.

'Guess I'm gonna have to go back.'

He looked across at Applejack, shaking his head in an effort to clear his head of its preoccupations.

'What do you mean? Go back where?'

'Go back to Drugget and the Triangle S.'

'Why would you do that? You said yourself that he was already suspicious about you. After this he'll be certain you ain't playin' him straight.'

'It's Quinn I need to worry about at the moment, and he ain't likely to put in an appearance at the

98

Triangle S until they all come together for the robbery. With any luck, I should be OK. I've been thinkin' it over and, despite what you said, it seems to me the only way we're gonna find out where that robbery is goin' to take place.'

'It's too dangerous,' Cooley replied. 'There's other ways we can work it out.'

'Maybe so, maybe not. The only way we're gonna know for certain is by gettin' the information from the horse's mouth. And remember, we ain't got time to go beatin' about the bush. We got to get that information real quick.'

'There's no guarantee you'll be able to find out. Even if you do, how are you gonna pass it on?'

The oldster considered for a moment.

'I don't know,' he concluded. 'We'll just have to play it by ear. I know where to find you. If I can get the information, I'll get the message to you somehow.'

Cooley shook his head.

'I don't like it,' he said.

'Hell, I don't like it either,' Applejack replied. 'But can you think of anythin' better? The main thing I'm gonna have to worry about is Quinn gettin' back to the Triangle S before me. That ain't likely, mainly because he'll be lookin' for you. If I can get straight back there, I should have some time.'

'You're right about Quinn. I wonder if there's anythin' I can do to keep him up here, delay his return long enough for you to try and find out what we need to know?'

'How would you do that?'

'I don't know. Maybe lead him on some way. Make him think he's on to me.' The fire was burning low.

'Get some shut-eye,' Cooley said. 'I'll sit up on guard awhile. I need to think.' The oldster spread out his bed-roll.

'I'll get off early in the mornin',' he said.

Starr Schandler rode into town and, dismounting, tied his horse to the hitch-rack outside the marshal's office. The first thing his eyes met was a poster on the wall displaying a fair likeness to old Applejack. Quickly, he scanned the wording:

Wanted for murder and robbery of the bank at Little Fork.
$500 dollar reward for arrest or capture.

He knocked on the door and without waiting for a reply, stepped inside. Baines was sitting on a chair with his feet on the table. When he entered, the deputy marshal swung his legs down and stood up.

'Mr Schandler,' he said. 'What a pleasure. We don't get to see you too often.'

'The Triangle S takes up most of my time,' Schandler replied.

He looked around him. The marshal's office was bare of furniture apart from the chair and the desk and a rack on the wall with a rifle. There was a door behind the table which led to two cells.

'I understand you've had some trouble,' he said.

100

The deputy marshal nodded.

'Bank robbery,' he confirmed. 'They got away with near enough twenty thousand dollars, mainly in gold and government bonds. Two people got killed – the bank manager and an elderly lady used to run the Old Bennington café.'

'Terrible,' Schandler murmured.

'Trust me, they won't get away with it. You saw the poster outside?'

'Sure did. Looks like you got a good description.'

'Yeah, a real lucky break. Seems the man's bandanna slipped and a young fella got a clear view of his face.'

'It says he was the one did the killin'.'

'He was there. That's good enough for me.'

'Yeah. Now look here. We can't have this sort of thing happenin' to decent folks. These renegades must be found, and if it might help, I'd like to contribute another five hundred dollars to that reward you're advertisin'.'

He felt inside his coat and produced a leather wallet. Out of it he shook a number of bills.

'Take it right now,' he said.

Surprise showing on his face, the deputy marshal hesitantly accepted the money.

'That's a real fine gesture,' he said, 'and I'll make sure the townsfolk get to know about it.'

Schandler shook his head and waved away the idea with a slight motion of the hand.

'Don't worry about that. Just make sure you put these *hombres* behind bars.' He turned as if to go.

'This young fella, what did you say his name was? I take it he'll make a good witness?'

'Melvin Lake,' the marshal answered. 'Clarence Lake's boy. He's been working at Sam Tench's general store.'

'It must have been a very traumatic experience.'

Schandler moved to the door and opened it.

'Let me know if there's anything else I can do,' he said.

He stepped out into the sunshine and, with a glance up and down the street, moved to his horse and climbed into the saddle. He rode at a walking pace but once he was outside of town he dug in his spurs. When he got back to the Triangle S, Cage Drugget was leaning back in his chair on the porch, a cigar in his mouth and a glass of bourbon on a small table at his side. He looked pleased with himself. Schandler dismounted and as one of the hands led the horse to the stable, walked up the steps of the veranda.

'Well?' Drugget snapped.

'Seems like Marshal Cooley is out of town at the moment. He's left his deputy in charge.'

'Never mind that. What did Baines have to say about the bank job?'

'Seems like they got a suspect. There's a Wanted poster right outside the marshal's office.'

'Didn't take them long,' Drugget said. 'Was it the old man?'

Schandler nodded.

'Sure is. That boy must have given them a real

good description. There's no mistaking him. It's old Applejack all right.'

Drugget's mouth curled in an ugly grin.

'Maybe I was wrong to suspect him after all,' he said.

Schandler hesitated, uncertain whether the interview was over or not. Drugget made no indication that it wasn't so he turned and began to walk away towards the bunkhouse. It hadn't been but a brief while since it had been him drinking the whiskey and enjoying the cigars, he reflected. He felt a sudden surge of anger but he knew better than to allow his resentment to show. Drugget was back and there wasn't anything he could do about it. At least, not for the moment. At some stage an opportunity to alter the situation might present itself. In the meantime, however, he had no choice but to accept the new status quo: not if he wanted to stay alive.

CHAPTER FIVE

It was still early morning when Applejack rode into the yard of the Triangle S, having set off before dawn. He had no way of knowing if Quinn and the rest of his boys had got back to the ranch before him, but he figured it was more likely that they were still out in the oxbow lake region or even looking for Cooley in the Indian Breaks country. It would certainly make things easier for him if they were and he had no fears about the marshal's ability to look after himself. He stepped down from the leather and led his horse to the stables. There didn't seem to be anybody about so when he had tended to it he made his way to the bunkhouse. Some of Drugget's men were in there. A couple of them acknowledged him with a nod or a grunt.

'You ain't seen Quinn about?' he inquired.

'Nope. Thought he was with you.'

'I left to come back down here.'

'The boss is still not too happy about the way that

bank job went. Maybe Quinn ain't in such a hurry to get back.'

'I'm lookin' for Drugget. Is he around?'

'So far as I know, he's in the ranch house.'

There was no point in further delay. The oldster crossed the yard and knocked on the ranch house door. It was opened by Drugget himself.

'Well, if it ain't old Applejack,' he said. 'I been expectin' you back with Quinn and the boys.'

'Quinn's right behind me. I come on ahead 'cause I got some information you might be interested in.'

Drugget stepped aside.

'Come right on in. I figure you could use a shot of bourbon.'

The oldster took a seat while Drugget poured the drinks. When they had been set down and he had taken a swig, Drugget looked at him inquiringly.

'Well, what you got to say to me? What's this information you're talkin' about?'

Applejack took another drink. He could see no reason not to mention Cooley's name. It was information Quinn would soon supply, and of no use to Drugget anyway.

'It's about the marshal,' he said. 'I think he might be on to us.'

'And why do you think that?'

'He put in an appearance up by the oxbow lake. I'm wonderin' whether he managed to find our sign and track us that far.'

'If he has, Quinn will take care of him.'

Applejack nodded.

'Yeah, I guess so. I just thought you might like to know.'

Drugget sat down on a sofa.

'You did the right thing,' he said. 'But you don't need to worry about Cooley. Me and him go back a ways. I got a score to settle and I got it all under control.'

Applejack didn't want to push his luck, but he had come to try and find out the where the next robbery was being planned so there was no point in holding back. He would just have to risk Drugget's suspicions.

'I know none of us have to worry now you're back in charge,' he said. 'Man, it sure feels good to be back in business again.'

Drugget gave a short, cruel laugh.

'You might be an old goat,' he said, 'but you're a game one.'

'Gettin' back with you and the gang is like having the years roll back. Say, have you decided which bank we knock over yet? I'm about ready for more action.'

'Haven't you had enough already? Hell, you ain't hardly had time to recover yet from the last one.'

'I guess it's just kinda whetted my appetite.'

Their glasses were empty. Drugget got to his feet again and refilled them.

'Gladstone Notch,' he said.

Applejack took a slow sip of the whiskey before raising his eyes and looking Drugget steadily in the eye. Drugget returned the look.

'It's gonna be the bank at Gladstone Notch,' he repeated.

Their gaze held a moment longer but Applejack's features remained impassive.

'Gladstone Notch,' he said. 'That's a fair ride.'

'Three days' time,' Drugget said. 'There's a big shipment of gold comin' in on the overland stage.'

'Why not hit the stage?'

'Because we don't know exactly which one it's goin' to be on. But I got it on good information that it's gonna be there by Friday.'

Applejack grinned.

'You sure got things tagged,' he said.

He finished his drink and stood up.

'Don't say anythin' to the boys yet,' Drugget said. 'I'll be holdin' a meetin' later.'

He escorted the oldster to the door.

'Make sure you stick around,' he concluded.

When the oldster had ridden off, Cooley sat by the dwindling fire and finished off his breakfast. The first rays of dawn were lightening the sky when he climbed into the saddle. As he did so, his shoulder began to hurt again. Ignoring it, he urged the horse forwards. He had no plan in mind other than what he had arranged with the oldster: to come up with something which might delay the departure of Quinn and his boys for the Triangle S. It seemed to him that the best way to do this would be to expose his presence to Quinn and then lead him in a chase, making sure to keep just ahead of the game. He was confident of his own ability to elude the gunmen and was encouraged, too, by the thought that Drugget would not want him dead just yet. If he was right about Drugget, that gentleman would want to savour his revenge and carry it out personally. It might be a feather in Quinn's cap to bring him in, but he would have to be careful about the way he did it. On the other hand, Quinn was possibly not the man to think rationally and any of the other gunnies might be tempted to take a shot. How many of them were fully aware of Drugget's intentions towards him? Presumably he had given them some indication, but on the other hand he seemed to have a lot of men at his disposal and not all of them were likely to be briefed. It was a risk he would have to take.

He rode steadily back in the direction of the oxbow lake, confident of being able to pick up the gunnies' trail. When he reached the place where he had had the shootout, the bodies were gone. There was plenty of sign and he could read from it that a couple of riders had set off back in the direction of the shacks while the others, maybe four of them, had continued their pursuit of him. They had veered in a wrong direction, probably confused by Applejack's trail. That was an indication that they had no expert tracker amongst them. The security which he and Applejack had enjoyed the night before seemed to confirm the fact. After examining the sign, he climbed back into the saddle and began to ride in the wake of the four riders who had been following him. It struck him what an odd situation it was. They were playing a game of hide and seek in which the roles were liable to reverse. One thing he was thankful for was that the gunslicks had not all gone back to the shacks. They had carried on in their pursuit of him. That gave the oldster more of the time he needed. As long as Quinn was occupied with seeking him, the less the danger for old Applejack.

He hadn't gone far when he came upon the remains of a camp-fire. Getting down from his horse, he examined it closely. The ashes were still warm and there had been little attempt made at concealing it. What concerned him, however, was that it hadn't been made by the gunnies. Their tracks passed nearby but there was only one set of hoof prints around the camp-fire itself. The ground had been churned up by only one pair of boots. Drawing himself erect, Cooley looked about him. There were some scattered rocks and patches of bushes which might conceal a man or a horse; he was quick to remount and move away. He carried on, following the faint trail left by whoever it was had built the camp. He expected it to lead back towards the main trail left by the gunnies, on the assumption that it had been made by one of their number, but instead it veered away in the direction of the river. He brought his horse to a halt, trying to decide on what he should do next. His main purpose was to find Quinn and his men and trick them into following him. On the other hand, he was beginning to be intrigued by the sign of the lone rider that he had found. He had ridden out of the rougher country and was down in the flatlands surrounding the river. From time to time he could see the sweep of it glistening in the distance but the route he was following seemed to be bringing him closer to its banks where it took a wide loop. He was approaching a grove of cypress trees. When he was amongst them he dropped from the saddle and, taking his rifle, tethered the horse to a tree before moving forward on foot. He had not seen anything, but the tracks he was following seemed to lead into the cypress grove and he wasn't taking any chances. Keeping close to the shelter of the trees, he crept on. After a short distance the trees thinned and he could see the glimmer of water. He carried on till he was on the edge of the tree cover and had a good view of the river-bank. There was a man standing beside the water with his back to him. There was no sign of his horse; Cooley guessed it was back in the trees. The man was smoking a cigarette and was completely unaware of Cooley. He carried on smoking and looking across the river towards the opposite bank. When the cigarette was finished he flicked it into the water and slowly turned.

Cooley felt a cold hand clutch at his chest and his scalp tingled. It was all he could do not to gasp out loud. The man was quite close and he had a clear view. He recognized those features; they were quite distinctive, but it wasn't possible. The features were those of Belinda's father, the man he had buried! He felt panic seize him and a sickening dread. He was not afraid to face his enemies, but this was something different. This was not a living person, but a ghost, a wraith, an apparition. He felt his gorge rise and then

110

the rifle dropped from his fingers. The apparition heard the noise and quickly turned. Its eyes stared into those of Cooley. Cooley was transfixed as fear and revulsion swept through him like a wave. Then the apparition reached into its belt and produced a revolver and the spell was broken. Even in his shattered state, Cooley was sufficiently aware to know that ghosts don't usually carry six-guns. Instinctively he reached for his own side-irons but stopped as he realized the apparition had the drop on him.

'Hold it right there!' the man said.

Cooley raised his arms.

'Step forward and take your gun-belt off. Throw it on the ground. And do it real slow.'

Cooley emerged from the trees on to the river-bank, unbuckled his gun-belt and dropped it as the man commanded. When he had done so the man took a step forward and kicked it further aside.

'Now, sit down.'

Cooley dropped to the ground. He was still shaken but beginning to recover some of his composure. The stranger was taking on the lineaments of a man and not a spectre. The man continued to point his gun towards him but his stern attitude seemed to soften.

'I know who you are,' the man said.

Cooley found his voice.

'Ain't tryin' to keep it a secret,' he said.

'You're Rupe Cooley, marshal of Little Fork.'

'So?'

He was feeling surer of himself by the second.

'There's somethin' about you seems mighty familiar too,' he said, 'but I got grave doubts about just
what it is.'

The shadow of a smile played about the man's lips.

'Look,' he said, 'I don't figure I'll be needin' this.'

He twirled the gun once and then slid it beneath
his belt.

'Let me introduce myself,' he continued. 'The
name's Chesterton, Curt Chesterton. I'm Miss
Belinda Chesterton's uncle.'

Cooley let out a low sigh of relief. The matter was
clear to him now. The man in front of him was the
brother of the man he had buried. The resemblance
was remarkable.

'This is all a bit dramatic,' the man said. 'I just
couldn't afford to take any chances. Stand up and get
your guns. I think I've got a bit of explaining to do.'

Cooley retrieved his weapons and when they sat
together, offered the other man his tobacco pouch.
They built smokes and Cooley leaned back against a
tree trunk. He had a sudden insight into the question which had been troubling him.

'It weren't you, by any chance, who took a pot shot
at me in Little Fork?' he said.

Chesterton nodded shamefacedly.

'I'm afraid it was. I hope you can find it in yourself
to forgive me. I feel so ashamed. I must have been
out of my head with grief. You see, I came out to
meet my brother and Belinda. I found the wagon. It
was pretty obvious what had happened. When I saw
you with her in town I jumped to conclusions. I

assumed you were the person responsible.'

'You can't have been thinkin' too clearly,' Cooley replied.

'I got to talkin' with some men in the Blue Horse Saloon. They didn't paint a very good picture of you. It was only later I learned better.'

He was obviously finding it difficult to go on so Cooley concentrated on his cigarette, not saying anything and giving Chesterton time to compose himself. After a short interval Chesterton spoke again in a steadier voice.

'Tell me,' he said, 'is Belinda OK?'

'Yes, she's doin' fine. As a matter of fact, she's stayin' with my sister.'

'Then I'll be able to see her?'

'Don't see why not. I got some business to finish first, though.'

Cooley gave Chesterton a brief account of events.

'So this man Drugget is responsible for what happened to my brother?' Chesterton asked when he had finished. 'When I got to seein' straight, I kinda figured there was a lot more to all this. That's why I followed your trail when I realized you'd left town. I lost track of it. I think I was hopin' you might find me.'

He paused to inhale.

'This *hombre* Drugget sounds a real bad number. If I can make up for takin' that shot at you in any way, I'd be only too happy. You can count on my gun bein' right behind you.'

'Maybe that's what I should be worryin' about,'

Cooley replied.

Chesterton glanced at him and then they both laughed.

'You were a terrible shot,' Cooley said. 'To be honest, I'm not sure how much help you'd be.'

He stopped to think for a moment.

'Maybe there is something,' he replied.

'Just tell me. I mean what I say about wantin' to make it up. Besides, I got a stake in this after what Drugget did to my brother and Belinda.'

'I told you old Applejack has gone back to the Triangle S to try and find out what Drugget's got planned. Problem is, even if he finds out, we ain't come up with a good way for him to get the information back to me.'

'Consider the matter solved,' Chesterton responded. 'Drugget doesn't know me. Why don't I ride right on to the Triangle S myself and establish contact with this man Applejack?'

'What excuse are you goin' to have for turnin' up at the Triangle S?'

'It doesn't matter. I'll think of something.'

Cooley pondered.

'I wasn't meanin' for you to take that sort of risk,' he said.

'Well, if it's a risk, it's a risk I'm happy to take. Don't think any more of it. Once we've finished here I'll head straight off. You carry on and do whatever you need to do with Quinn and I'll meet up with you back in town.'

Cooley was about to reply when his ears picked up

the sound of hoof beats.

'What is it?' Chesterton said, seeing the look on his face.

'I think we might have business with Quinn quicker than we thought,' he replied. 'Listen!'

They both strained their ears to pick up the tell-tale sound: there was no mistaking the fact that a bunch of riders was coming their way.

'You figure it's the gunslicks?'

'Who else would it be? Where's your horse? You got it hidden?'

'She's back among the trees. I doubt anyone would find her unless they were lookin' for her. You think we should ride away from here?'

'We probably should,' Cooley replied. 'But I'm getting' kinda tired of Quinn and the rest of 'em. What do you say we deal with him right now? That way old Applejack ain't gonna have worries about them turnin' up at the Triangle S.'

'I'm with you,' Chesterton said. 'I'll be grateful for the chance to be doin' somethin' to get back at those varmints.'

They both got quickly to their feet.

'Follow me,' Cooley said. 'We'll make our way through the trees and be ready for them as they approach the river.'

Without further delay, they slipped through the trees till they reached the opposite side where they had a view over the surrounding country.

'How do you know where they're gonna come out?' Chesterton said.

'They'll have found our tracks. Remember, I followed yours. Chances are, they'll come right on here.'

They took position behind a stand of cypress trees and checked their weapons. The sound of the approaching horsemen had faded while they were among the trees but before long the changing breeze carried the dull rumble of galloping hoofs to their ears once more. Cooley glanced across at Chesterton. He wasn't sure what to expect from him, how he might shape up. Chesterton nodded and tipped him a wink. He seemed to be OK. It was irrelevant anyway because, having made the decision to stand and fight, there was nothing he could do to change it now.

The first of the riders appeared slightly ahead of the rest, and Cooley recognized him at once as Quinn. Just behind him the others were slightly strung out; a group of three, then another single rider, and then two more; seven in all. It was more than Cooley had anticipated. Either Quinn had been joined by some others, or there had been more of them back at the shacks than he had allowed for. Given that most of his men were at the Triangle S, it was certainly true that Drugget had plenty of men he could call on. It made it all the more urgent and necessary to put a stop to his activities before he became even more powerful. He already controlled the Triangle S and was on the verge of gaining control over other ranches in the area. The town of Little Fork was beginning to feel his influence. What it all meant was that finding out exactly where Drugget intended to strike next was crucial. If Drugget got away with this next job, he would have the where-withal to do as he pleased. He had to be stopped.

Quinn had slowed slightly and the others were catching him up. Cooley expected him to carry on riding right into the trees and he seemed to be doing just that when he drew his horse to a sudden stop. He shouted something and the riders began to spread out. They must have seen something. Cooley glanced sideways and it was obvious what had happened: whether by accident or design, Chesterton had partly emerged from cover. Cooley didn't have time to do or say anything as bullets began to crash into the trees, sending up shards and splinters of bark and ripping branches from the canopy. He expected Chesterton to get back under cover but to his con-sternation he began to move forward into the open. His six-guns were in his hands and he was firing from both barrels as he walked. The gunslicks were gener-ally aiming too high but as some of them began to slide from their saddles and take whatever cover they could, their aim became more accurate. Cooley shouted to Chesterton but his words were lost in the cacophony of noise. Slowly and steadily, Chesterton continued to advance, his guns flaming. All Cooley could do was to provide some covering support and he began to blaze away with the rifle. A number of men and horses had gone down and Cooley's fire was proving effective. Still Chesterton stepped forward. He was completely exposed but he seemed to lead a charmed life.

A couple of the gunnies wheeled their horses and began to ride away as Chesterton continued his relentless advance. For all the effect the gunnies' fire was having, Chesterton might as well have been the wraith Cooley had initially taken him to be. Cooley had an uncomfortable feeling that perhaps he had been right all along. He had to make a conscious effort to rid his head of the uncanny sensation. His rifle was hot in his hands but he was out of ammunition. Throwing it down, he pulled out his Colts and began to pour lead in the direction of the gunslicks. His view of what was happening was obscured by a drifting cloud of gun smoke and when it cleared a little he could not see Chesterton any more. He continued firing but suddenly he was aware that the noise of gunfire had ceased. He was the only one still firing. He stopped, and the silence which ensued was broken only by the diminishing sound of hoof beats. The last of the remaining gunnies was fast disappearing from sight. He looked about for Chesterton and after a moment saw him stretched out on the grass a good twenty yards in front of him. When he was confident that there was nothing more to fear from the gunslicks he stepped out and rapidly covered the ground between him and the recumbent form of Chesterton. He feared the worst. It seemed impossible that anybody could have walked unscathed through that storm of gunfire and survived. Chesterton was lying face down. Carefully, Cooley turned him over. The man's eyes were closed and blood was running down his face. Cooley was about to lay him flat again when Chesterton's eyes unexpectedly opened. After all that had happened, Cooley was feeling jumpy and he flinched. A slow grin spread across Chesterton's features.

'So I'm still alive,' he said. 'Have I been hit?'

Cooley began to examine him more closely. There was no sign of injury apart from a line of white across the side of the man's skull.

'You've been lucky,' he said. 'As far as I can see, a bullet's creased your hairline but otherwise you're OK. Another fraction of an inch and that would have been all she wrote.'

Chesterton struggled into a sitting posture, wincing as he did so.

'Hell, my head's poundin',' he said.

'That was a plumb crazy thing you did,' Cooley said. 'What in tarnation were you playin' at?'

Chesterton began to shake his head but immediately groaned with pain.

'I don't know,' he replied. 'Somethin' got into me. Seein' those murderin' varmints just made me mad. I guess I went kind of berserk.'

'Well, you seem to have driven them off pretty successfully. There ain't none of 'em hangin' around to argue the point.'

Cooley ripped off his bandanna and began to wipe the blood from Chesterton's face.

'Think you can get to your feet and walk?' he asked. 'I got a canteen of water and a flask of whiskey back in my saddle-bags.'

'Never mind the water. Just gimme the whiskey,'

Chesterton replied.

With Cooley's assistance, he struggled to his feet, his features contorted with pain as he did so.

'Wait a moment,' Cooley said. 'I guess I'd better just check on those gunnies.'

It took him only a matter of moments to confirm that five of the gunslicks had been killed. He looked especially for Quinn, but there was no sign of him. He must have been one of the two who got away. Three horses had been killed and the others had run off. Quickly, he returned to Chesterton and they made their way back through the trees to where Cooley had tethered his horse. Once a few slugs of whiskey had been poured down his throat, Chesterton began to feel noticeably better. Cooley made a rough and ready bandage from Chesterton's bandanna and wrapped it round his head, fastening it under his chin.

'You look like you just had a nasty experience with the big bad wolf,' he said, 'but it'll have to do.'

'Yeah, and you're a ringer for Little Red Riding Hood.'

Cooley left Chesterton with his horse while he went to find the man's mount. When he came back, he was sprawled on the grass.

'Are you OK?' he asked.

'Jut a bit of delayed shock, I guess. I suddenly felt kinda weak and my legs gave way.'

'That'll be the whiskey,' Cooley responded.

'Give me a hand to get up again.'

Cooley helped his companion back to his feet.

'Now, help me get on that horse.'

Cooley looked uncertain.

'Hell, I got to get to the Triangle S,' Chesterton said.

'You ain't in no fit state to ride,' Cooley replied.

'Remember what we were sayin' about Applejack. I got to get to the Triangle S and quick.'

'The situation's kinda different now, don't you think? Quinn won't be losin' any time headin' for the Triangle S. Besides, how are you gonna explain about that head wound?'

'Things happened pretty quickly. I don't reckon any of those gunnies had time to get a good look at me. They didn't manage to get very close. If Quinn beats me to it, chances are he won't recognize me.'

'That's a mighty big gamble,' Cooley said.

'Maybe, but it's one we got to take.'

'And what about that wound?'

'I'll take the bandage off. It won't look too bad. I can easily come up with some story.'

Cooley hesitated.

'Come on, we're wastin' time,' Chesterton said. 'Give me a hand up into the saddle.'

Cooley couldn't think of any better plan. Not without some difficulty, he hoisted Chesterton on to the horse's back.

'Get on to Little Fork and I'll see you there just as soon as I've got any information,' Chesterton said.

For a moment he swayed in the saddle but then righted himself and sat erect.

'*Adios,*' he said. 'See you in Little Fork.'

'I'll ride with you at least part of the way,' Cooley said.

Chesterton slowly shook his head.

'Better we go our separate ways. If Quinn's around, we don't want him to see us together.'

Cooley reflected for a moment.

'I guess you're right,' he said.

Without waiting further, Chesterton touched the horse's flanks with his spurs and moved off through the trees. Cooley watched until he vanished from sight and then climbed into leather himself. He was uncertain about what to do. The obvious thing was to simply head back for Little Fork but he felt reluctant to abandon Chesterton and Applejack. His inclination was to follow on Chesterton's trail and make for the Triangle S himself but reason told him that there was nothing he could do. Once he set foot on Triangle S property he would be recognized, in which case he would only make the situation worse rather than better. He would be playing straight into Drugget's hands and would do no favours to either Chesterton or Applejack by getting himself killed. He considered looking for Quinn but the gunslick had a good start on him and it was doubtful whether he would even be able to pick up his trail. One thing was for sure – Chesterton had proved his worth when it came to making a stand. He had more than made up for his lapse when he had attempted to shoot Cooley. Chesterton's keen sense of shame and guilt had probably been instrumental in driving him to act as he had. He was certainly no back-stabber or drygulcher. And he was Belinda's uncle. The thought of Belinda acted like a tonic to Cooley's tired and frazzled condition. Thinking of her, he set his course for Little Fork.

It was late in the day. Melvin Lake, having finished his day's work at the general store, was walking down the quiet street towards his house. He did not notice two men walking behind him. They were hard looking and wearing tied-down guns. Melvin was feeling happier than he had for some time. Since his conversation with Cooley he had been thinking a lot about what the marshal had said. They seemed to open fresh possibilities for him.

'All right, kid!' a voice snarled. 'This is just about far enough.'

Melvin spun round. He became aware for the first time of the two men behind him. They had drawn their Walker Colts and were pointing them right at him.

'Time to say your prayers,' the man said.

His partner laughed.

'Yeah, we got a little something for you.'

Melvin froze. He was unable to make any sense of their remarks.

'Turn round and keep walkin'.'

Melvin hesitated.

'Make it quick!' the man snapped.

Melvin did as he was bid. His back prickled and his legs began to shake. At any moment he expected the shot to come. He had just enough presence of mind to slow down, conscious of the fact they were only waiting to kill him till they were a suitable distance from the town centre. Otherwise he was barely in a frame of mind to register the sound of a voice suddenly calling to him.

'Hit the deck, Melvin!'

Automatically he threw himself forwards and sideways. Almost at the same instant shots rang out from behind him and he felt the singing of lead as it flew overhead. From somewhere further behind him a man had stepped forward. Crouching, he began to fire at the two gunslicks, fanning the gun with rapid movements of his free palm. From the corner of his eye Melvin saw the two men crumple backwards and fall. One of them struggled to his feet and began to stagger towards the newcomer before a single shot tore into his chest and he fell. It had all happened in an instant. Melvin rose to his feet and looked at the man who was approaching him, his smoking gun in his hand. For a moment he did not recognize him, and then he saw it was Deputy Marshal Baines.

'Never fire a gun like that,' Baines said with a grin. 'Except in an emergency.'

Melvin was bemused.

'I figure those two no-good skunks were out to silence you about the robbery,' Baines said. 'You are the only witness.'

'How can I thank you?' Melvin began.

'No need for thanks. In fact, I think I owe you an apology. I should have been aware of the danger you might have placed yourself in. I should have taken steps to protect you.'

Melvin felt himself begin to shake.

'Come on,' the deputy marshal said. 'Let's get you safely back home. You've nothing to fear now. I'll see about those two later.'

CHAPTER SIX

When Marshal Cooley rode into Little Fork, almost the first person he saw was Belinda Chesterton. She was just coming out of Eliza Dodd's millinery shop with a big hatbox under her arm. He came alongside her and drew his horse to a halt. She looked up at him.

'Mr Cooley,' she said, 'you weren't supposed to see this. It was meant to be a surprise.'

'Can't see nothin' but a box,' he replied.

He stepped down from the saddle.

'Actually, I bought myself a hat because I was feeling low,' Belinda continued.

'It's been a hard time for you,' he replied.

He was about to tell her that he had met her uncle but then thought better of it. He didn't want to get involved in a lot of explanations at the present time. She looked at him more closely and for the first time noticed how tired and drawn his features were.

'Seein' you back in Little Fork is enough,' she said.

'How are things?' he asked.

'If you mean, how's your sister, she's just fine. In fact we're meeting for coffee at the hotel. Why don't you join us?'

'I got some business with Baines,' he said. 'It won't take long. You two have coffee and I'll see you back at the house.'

She made an effort to appear impassive.

'Where have you been?' she asked. 'We've both been worried about you.'

'I'll tell you about it later.'

He swung back into the saddle and rode the short distance to the marshal's office where he got back down and tied the horse to the hitchrack. He glanced over his shoulder just in time to see Belinda disappear through the doorway of the hotel. He had wanted to say more to her but had been taken off-guard. She certainly looked good, even better than he had remembered her. Involuntarily he turned his head towards the Old Bennington café. That was where Belinda and his sister would have met if old Miss Myres was alive. The thought steeled him; with gritted teeth he opened the door of his office and stepped inside, pausing for just a moment to glance at the Wanted poster for old Applejack.

Baines was standing at the stove.

'I saw you comin' down the street,' he said. 'Figured you might appreciate some coffee.'

'Sure do,' Cooley answered. 'If you look in that bottom drawer, I think you'll find somethin' to give it a bit of a kick.'

He sat down at his desk and Baines pulled up a

chair beside him.

'Anythin' been happenin' since I been gone?' Cooley asked.

'I had a visit from Schandler. I wouldn't have given it much thought but he seemed a mite curious about Melvin Lake. He wanted to make a contribution towards the reward money.'

'Sounds a bit suspicious.'

'Yeah, that's what I thought, especially after what you'd said about the Triangle S. It kinda put me on my guard. Yesterday I had to rescue Melvin from a bit of a run-in with a couple of mean coyotes. Their corpses are still at the undertaker's if you want to take a look at 'em.'

'I'd be willin' to bet they're from the Triangle S. You done good.'

'I should have done better but it turned out OK. What about you?'

In as few words as possible, Cooley sketched in the outline of what had happened to him since leaving town.

'So old Applejack is playing a double role,' Baines ejaculated when he had finished. 'He's a sly old fox. Who would have expected it?'

'We can take that Wanted poster off the wall,' Cooley replied.

'Are you quite sure you can trust the old codger?' Baines said.

'Yeah, I'm sure.'

Cooley didn't add that he was confident, too, of his deputy. Circumstances and appearance could lead a man astray. He had been wrong to have any doubts about either Applejack or Baines. Over the years he had come to rely on his own instincts and he knew he should have trusted them all along. Applejack and Baines were sound. He knew he could count on them when the showdown came.

Whatever it was he had meant to say to Belinda, it remained unspoken that evening when he got back to the house. Although he knew there was little chance of Chesterton getting back to him with any information that day, he still felt the need to be at his office. It was Baines who finally persuaded him to go back home. It was late and he felt exhausted. It took him some time to stable the horse and attend to its needs and he was only part-way through when he heard footsteps and turned round to see his sister.

'You're late,' she said. 'We expected you a lot earlier.'

She came over to him and he took her in his arms and kissed her.

'You know how it is,' he said.

'No, I don't. Not really. You spend too much time doing the job. If it's going to take up so much of your time, maybe you should think of deputizing one or two more of the townsfolk.'

'Maybe you're right,' he said. 'Maybe I'll do that, though it'll be hard to find anyone as good as Baines.'

She helped him attend to the horse, talking as she did so.

'You know Miss Belinda has been really concerned about you?' she said. He didn't reply.

'Well, she has.'

She paused before continuing.

'You know, she's a lovely girl. I've really enjoyed her being around. I didn't realize just how much I missed having some company when you're not there.'

Cooley hung his saddle over a peg on the wall.

'I gather you and she had coffee in town earlier?'

'Yes. I think she was disappointed you didn't join us.'

'I would have, but I needed to see Baines.'

He had his back to her and didn't see her shake her head.

'One day,' she said, 'you'll realize what's important. There's other things besides doing your job.'

He stroked his hand over the horse's muzzle.

'That's about it,' he said. 'Come on, let's go inside.'

Despite the best efforts of his sister and Belinda, he could not settle down. Though he tried not to show it, he was restless and couldn't concentrate properly on anything other than what might be happening at the Triangle S. He began to have fresh doubts about the plan of action that had been decided on, first with Applejack and then with Chesterton. It had been remiss of him to put their lives in danger. It was he who should be taking the risks. He was almost tempted to saddle his horse once more and ride out to the Triangle S but his better judgement told him that it would serve no

130

purpose. If anything, he would only put them all in more danger by doing so. There was nothing to do except to wait, but it was very difficult.

When the two women departed to their rooms for the night, he stayed downstairs and, turning down the lamps, sat in the dark going over and over everything that had happened. The ticking of the clock seemed to grow louder and louder. It seemed to ring in his ears so he got to his feet and walked out on to the veranda. He leaned on the rail looking out into the night. The bedrooms above him were dark and he was distracted by thoughts of Belinda lying there so close to him. He sat down on a cane chair and rolled a cigarette but after a few drags he stubbed it out. He stood by the rail once more. The night was still. Only once the bark of a dog briefly broke the silence and then it was quiet again. The town of Little Fork lay sleeping but he knew the calm was deceptive. Only the gun strapped to his side kept it that way. So it would be till the land was sufficiently tamed for the rule of law to be the arbitrator in men's quarrels. In the meantime he had a job to do and another battle to face – the biggest of his life. He just had to keep patient and wait for the word that would set it all in motion: if it ever came.

Dawn had scarcely broken before he was back in his office. The streets were dark and deserted. Only a dim lamp glowed in an occasional window. The poster of old Applejack had been taken down from the wall of the building and been thrown into a waste paper basket.

'Coulda saved the effort of printing it,' he reflected.

He didn't imagine that having the poster on display had contributed to saving the oldster's life. He made some breakfast and when he had finished he stood by the window, peering through the blinds. It was still early but the town was beginning to stir. Jim Dalton was sweeping the boardwalk outside his grocery store and the big door of Morgan's Livery and Feed stood open. A light came on in Sam Tench's window and Cooley expected to see young Melvin Lake make an appearance shortly. He turned and cleared away his plate and mug before sitting down at the desk. Then he got to his feet and, taking the keys from a hook on the wall, opened the door leading to the empty cells. He stood for a moment looking about him before walking back through to the general office where he hung up the keys once more. He went back to look out of the window. A few more people had appeared, people he knew, going about their daily business. A cat appeared, slinking along the opposite side of the street. It stopped and began to roll in the dust. A corner of Cooley's mouth lifted in the suggestion of a smile as the cat walked on to disappear round the corner of a building.

He turned his head away and saw the figure of Baines at the far end of the street. He was walking slowly and twice he touched the brim of his hat to folk he met. Cooley wondered if he had passed half as restless a night as he had. He guessed not. Baines wasn't aware of all the ramifications of the situation and he didn't carry the weight of responsibility Cooley felt for Applejack and Chesterton. Chesterton's being Belinda's uncle made it personal. Baines didn't know Drugget either, like Cooley did. He certainly appeared to be relaxed. Cooley stepped aside as he came to the door and entered.

'Howdy,' he said. 'I thought I was early. How long have you been here?'

'I couldn't sleep,' Cooley replied.

'Any of that coffee left?'

'Sure. Help yourself.'

The presence of Baines helped to calm Cooley's nerves. The two of them sat and talked in desultory fashion for a time. Cooley got the impression that maybe he was wrong about the deputy's state of mind. His conversation was more general, more vague. He had a feeling that they were both talking to fill in the time, to keep something at bay.

Time crawled along. Every so often Cooley glanced at the clock on the wall and walked to the window to peer out. The town was fully awake now and going about its business. A few horses were tethered to the various hitch posts and a wagon passed by, lumbering down the street. The sun glinted from shop windows and when he looked up, he could see a few white clouds drift above the roofs of the clapboard buildings. Just out of the corner of his eye he had a glimpse of the white tower of the church raising itself towards the heavens.

'That coyote Quinn must have made it back to the Triangle S before now,' Baines commented. 'You figure Applejack's alibi will stand up?'

A nerve twitched in Cooley's cheek.

'I wish I'd got on the trail of that varmint and hunted him down,' he said.

It was the first time either of them had made any reference to the situation that was occupying both of their minds.

'I been wonderin' about that gold Applejack had with him when he came into town. Do you reckon it was real?'

Cooley let out a low laugh.

'It would be just like the old jackass to have some gold dust stored away, but I figure it was fool's gold.'

'Why would he carry it with him?'

'Applejack is pretty cunning. He probably persuaded Drugget that he knew where to find gold.'

'To kind of boost his standing with the gang?'

'Yeah. Seems he once rode the owlhoot trail but Drugget may still have wanted some kind of demonstration of his value to them. Remember, he let them in on the existence of those shacks beyond the oxbow lake. Anythin' that might make it worth their while to take him on could be useful.'

Cooley didn't say anything about Applejack's suspicions concerning the deputy marshal. After all, he had had his doubts about Baines himself.

Doubt and suspicion seemed to hang in the atmosphere. As the hours ticked by Cooley began to suspect Chesterton's motives. Could he, after all, be in league with Drugget? Then he remembered the way Chesterton had conducted himself in the encounter with the gunslicks. That certainly wasn't the response of someone who might be associated with Drugget and his gang. If he hadn't shown up, it must mean that he had fallen foul of Drugget. In which case, it was Cooley's fault for having let him ride straight into a hornets' nest. Baines put more coffee on to boil.

'How about if I pop out and get us some food?' he asked.

'You get some if you want,' Cooley replied. 'I ain't feelin' hungry.'

'No, me neither,' Baines replied.

They drank more coffee and built smokes. Cooley continued to glance at the clock. He peered out of the window and then opened the door and went outside. He looked up and down the street. Suddenly he tensed. Coming into view he saw a rider and as he came closer he saw that it was Chesterton. There was no sign of the oldster.

'Baines!' he called. 'Chesterton's here!'

The deputy marshal tumbled from his chair and joined Cooley on the boardwalk. Coming alongside them, Chesterton drew his horse to a halt.

'Cooley,' he said, 'it's good to see you.'

'We were gettin' worried. What kept you so long?'

Without waiting for a reply, Baines invited Chesterton inside and poured some of the black coffee into a tin mug.

'Guess you could use some of this,' he said.

Chesterton sat down and took a long sip.

'Hell, that's good,' he said.

While he was drinking, Cooley made the introductions. When the cup was empty, Chesterton sighed and turned to the marshal. Cooley's face was lined with tension.

'What happened?' he snapped. 'What about old Applejack?'

'He's OK, but there was no way he could get away. I didn't get to meet Drugget. I told his foreman, Schandler, that I was lookin' for a job. He said they didn't need anyone and I'd better get off the Triangle S as quick as possible. I said that I was an acquaintance of a man called Applejack who would vouch for me. He wasn't interested but when I asked if I could have a word with the oldster he didn't seem to object. Your description was spot on. I only had a few minutes in the bunkhouse but I managed to convince Applejack that I was with you. I was hopin' he would be able to get away but he seemed to think it was too dangerous. I guess he didn't want to take the risk of gettin' us both into trouble.'

'That must have been yesterday. What took you so long?'

Chesterton's expression changed to one of grim determination.

'Seemed like Schandler must have had second thoughts. He came back to me saying there was a job he needed someone to help with, roustin' out a few cattle from some rough country on the far side of the range. It sounded suspicious but I had to go along with it. There was me and another cowhand and when we'd finished it was late and we had to put up at a line shack. This mornin' we were at it again. I had to wait for a chance to make a getaway; there were a few of Drugget's men around. I don't know what Schandler had in mind for me, but I don't think it was anythin' I'd appreciate.'

He stopped and glanced from Cooley to Baines.

'I found out what you wanted to know,' he said. 'Drugget aims to hit the bank at Gladstone Notch the day after tomorrow.'

'Gladstone Notch! I know the marshal there. I'll get a telegraph message off straight away.'

Chesterton shook his head.

'No need,' he said.

'What do you mean, no need?' Cooley snapped.

'Because there ain't no bank at Gladstone Notch. Leastways, not any more. There used to be but it closed.'

'So Drugget was tellin' Applejack a lie?'

'That's what it looks like.'

'So what do we do now?' Baines said. 'You're sure about what Applejack said?'

'Yeah. The bank at Gladstone Notch.'

Cooley began to pace the room.

'I got to try and figure this out,' he said.

'I've been thinkin',' Chesterton said, 'and if it's of any use to you, I'll tell you what I reckon.'

'Go ahead,' Cooley said. 'My head is so confused, I'd appreciate any ideas.'

'Well, there ain't no bank at Gladstone Notch. The nearest is Harpington. Gladstone Notch and Harpington are both on the stage line. What if that money is comin' in on the stage? And goin' to the bank at Harpington.'

Cooley paused.

'Yeah, you could be right. So Drugget could really be aimin' to rob the bank at Harpington?'

Chesterton paused for a moment.

'Or maybe he's aimin' to hold up the stagecoach and get his hands on the loot before it ever gets to the bank. I don't know. You're the marshal. Wouldn't it be easier for him to do that than to stage a bank robbery?'

Cooley pondered Chesterton's words.

'Hell, I think you got a point,' he said. 'It would be a lot less risky to hold up a stage than rob a bank.'

'There's still a possibility that it's the bank he's got in mind,' Baines interjected. 'And we got no way of knowin' for sure that it's either the bank at Harpington or the stagecoach.'

'That's true,' Cooley said, 'but we ain't got anythin' better to go on. Seems to me we're gonna have to take the chance that the stagecoach is the target. It's either that or nothin'.'

'Gladstone Notch is a good ride,' Baines remarked.

'Yeah, so I guess there ain't no point in hangin' around.'

'What about a posse?' Baines said.

'Ain't no time,' Cooley replied. 'Besides, nobody's committed a crime. It ain't as if we were ridin' after some *hombre*. It's just the three of us. Probably better that way.'

The grin had re-appeared on Chesterton's face.

'It's good enough for me,' he said. 'Why don't we get ridin'?'

It was around noon when Drugget and his gang saw the sign pointing in the direction of Gladstone Notch. They had taken a circuitous route, which led them to the narrow gap in the hills after which the town was named. Applejack, riding just behind Drugget and Quinn, was surprised that they hadn't come at the town more directly, but he couldn't afford to ask too many questions. He had been pushing his luck for some time and he couldn't be sure how much longer he was likely to get away with it. Drugget held up his hand and the riders came to a halt. Off in the distance the town lay spread-eagled in a shallow depression. Leading to it, the trail from Musgrove cut through the narrow pass.

'OK, men,' Drugget said. 'This is the place.'

There were more than fifteen riders. They looked about, a few with puzzled expressions.

'Some of you might have had the impression we were goin' to ride on into town and take the bank,' Drugget resumed. 'Well, we ain't. Not any more. Now I know for sure which stage that loot is comin' in on, it seems kinda sensible to lift it before it ever gets as far as the vault.'

'How did you find out?' someone shouted.

'I got friends in useful places,' Drugget replied. 'Like for instance the telegraph office.'

Someone hooted and a few of the men laughed.

'Yes,' Drugget continued, 'that stage should be passin' right by here in about two hours.'

'Plenty of time for us to take up position and get prepared,' Quinn said.

'Some of you take cover behind the rocks. Me and Quinn will stop the coach.' He turned to Applejack.

'You can come with us,' he said.

The oldster nodded. He suspected he was being set up for something but that was a minor concern compared with the way things were shaping up. He had been fooled. Drugget had convinced him that the hold-up was to be on the bank in Gladstone Notch and he had passed on that information. Whatever Marshal Cooley had in mind, any attempt now to foil Drugget would be doomed to failure. Cooley would be waiting at the wrong place. Applejack's brain raced. There was nothing he could do for the moment but to go along with Drugget. Something might turn up. In any event, he was on his own.

Following Drugget's instructions, the gunslicks spread out and took up their places behind rocks and patches of bush overlooking the trail. Drugget clambered down to the valley floor from where he looked up to check that his men were completely concealed. Then he, together with Quinn and Applejack, stationed themselves by the side of the trail.

'Give me your guns,' Drugget said to the oldster.

Applejack gave him a questioning look.

'Better do as he says,' Quinn said. He swung his rifle so it was pointed at the oldster.

'Won't I be needin' 'em?' Applejack said.

'Not for your role in this,' Drugget replied. 'Besides, we got plenty of men to deal with any opposition.'

Applejack started to say something in reply, but realized that there was no point in arguing. With a shrug of his shoulders he unbuckled his gun-belt and handed it to Drugget.

'Now, just step out into the road and lie down.'

'What's the point of that?' Applejack said.

'Don't argue,' Quinn snapped. 'Just do like the boss says.'

Drugget glanced at him.

'Oh, I don't know. I guess the old buzzard deserves an explanation.'

He turned to Applejack.

'When that stagecoach comes along it's likely to be goin' at a crackin' pace. We'll need to slow it down some. I thought about maybe puttin' a boulder in the way but then I had a better idea. A body lyin' across the track might be even more effective.'

Quinn gave an ugly laugh.

'But ain't it more likely to put the driver on the alert?' Applejack said desperately.

Drugget shrugged.

'Who knows? Makes no difference with all them boys watchin' up there.'

'Saves us a lot of trouble this way,' Quinn interposed. 'It could be mighty hard work gettin' a rock into position. This way, we don't have to do nothin'.'

It was Drugget's turn to laugh.

141

'You got to admit he's got a point,' he said.

'I reckon I'd be more use up behind those rocks like the rest of 'em,' Applejack replied.

Drugget's face suddenly darkened.

'That's enough talkin',' he snarled. 'Fact of the matter is, I don't trust you, old man. I ain't altogether sure which way that gun of yours is likely to be pointin' when it comes to the push. Look at the situation this way; you got a chance to show just how loyal you are.'

'You know I'm loyal. Why would I have come back and joined up with you again if I wasn't?'

Drugget laughed again.

'Now there's a question,' he said. 'Hell, I could think of a hundred reasons if I was ever to put my mind to it.'

He raised his own rifle.

'The stage should be here real soon. Now do as I say and stretch yourself out right where that stage-coach driver ain't gonna miss you.'

Applejack hesitated for a few moments; he glanced up at the slopes of the hill and then looked squarely into the muzzles of the two rifles that were pointed at him.

'OK,' he said. 'If that's the way you see it.'

He got to his feet and walked the dozen or so paces which took him into the centre of the trail, feeling horribly exposed as he did so. Then, with a final glance about him, he lay down in the dust.

'Sure looks like a goldurn dead coyote,' Quinn's voice shouted.

Applejack turned his head to take in as much of the scene as he could. Although he knew the gunslicks were all around the hillside, he could not see any of them. There were plenty places of concealment, and they had done a good job selecting them. The sun beat down; he felt completely vulnerable and he had an uncomfortable hollow sensation in the pit of his stomach. If one of those gunslicks decided to take a shot at him, he was defenceless. His straining senses sought for the first distant rumblings of the stagecoach. Then he thought: what if some rider comes by first? But he knew the answer to that one. Drugget wouldn't hesitate to shoot dead any interloper. He wasn't going to let anything stand in his way now.

A long time seemed to pass before he felt rather than heard the approach of the stagecoach. It was nothing very precise; just the faintest intimation of a vibration in the ground. Slowly it gathered in strength till it became the unmistakable sound of hoof beats. He turned his head in the direction of the rocks behind which Drugget and Quinn were hiding, but there was nothing to indicate whether or not they had heard the approaching vehicle. The sound grew louder until it reached a level which none of the gunslicks could miss. Applejack's throat was dry and constricted. He could barely swallow. He contemplated getting to his feet but as if in answer to the thought the voice of Drugget rang out:

'Stay right where you are. One false move and you're dead.'

143

Applejack continued to lie still, realizing that it would make no difference to Drugget whether it was a live person or a corpse lying in the path of the stagecoach. Maybe he would be reluctant to fire in case the driver of the stage or the guard heard the shot, but it was unlikely that either of them would notice it above the thundering sound of the horses' hoofs and the stagecoach wheels. Whichever way you looked at it, Drugget held the whip hand. The complications he had introduced were for his own enjoyment. They were just a refinement. When all was said and done, he had more than enough men hidden on the hillsides to deal with the stagecoach. It was unlikely that the stage driver would see him and stop: Drugget would enjoy seeing him crushed and mangled beneath its wheels.

The din of hoofs was growing louder, but above the noise of the approaching stagecoach his ears picked up another sound, like a stinging of hailstones above a rolling thunderstorm. He couldn't imagine what it was but as he swivelled his eyes upwards he saw plumes of smoke on the mountainside. The sounds he had heard were the sounds of gunfire. His first assumption was that the gunslicks had commenced to fire on the stagecoach, but something told him that it was still too early. Despite the increasing levels of noise, his instinct was that the stage had not yet entered the defile. Then he heard shouting from close at hand.

'What the hell is goin' on?'

It was the voice of Quinn, but it was rapidly

drowned out by another burst of fire from the mountainside.

Taking advantage of the confusion, Applejack rolled to one side before quickly changing direction and rolling the other way. Dust rose into the air as bullets spattered into the earth where Applejack had been. The noise of the stagecoach now overwhelmed every other sound, and as Applejack got to his feet, the lead horse went crashing past so close that it brushed his side, sending him sprawling into the bushes. The coach was rattling along but when it had travelled a little way beyond where Applejack lay, it slowed down; flames and smoke appeared at the windows and then, as it came to a stop, a number of men leaped from its open doors, taking cover behind the stage. The horses were rearing and whinnying with fright. Applejack heard another voice shouting something and he assumed it was Quinn, but then he realized that it was coming from the direction of the coach. The next moment someone was scrambling towards him; as he approached he shouted again and threw a rifle.

'Start shootin', old timer!'

Gathering his scattered wits, Applejack recognized the familiar figure of Marshal Cooley. He picked up the rifle and began to fire towards the hillside from which plumes of smoke rose into the air, accompanied by the singing of lead. He had no time to ask any questions. The battle was raging and it was difficult to tell what was happening. Applejack glanced back to where Drugget and Quinn had concealed themselves. There was no smoke to indicate their presence. He looked behind him at the hillside and for a brief moment thought he saw a flash of colour. Without waiting further, he began to move up the hill, keeping low and making sure he kept under cover. The hillside opposite was obscured by a mass of smoke but on this side there seemed to be little action till a bullet shattered a rock near where he was crouching; it was rapidly followed by a second and a third shot. He lay still, watching for further signs of movement. Billows of smoke indicated where Drugget and Quinn must have taken up a fresh position and he loosed a couple of shots in their direction. He glanced behind him to where the stagecoach had come to a halt. For the first time he observed the writing along the top of the frame:

Wells, Fargo & Company

There were a number of people sheltering behind it and others seemed to have taken up positions on the hillside. Among those sheltering behind the coach he thought he recognized Baines and the man who had approached him at the Triangle S. What were they doing on the scene? He had provided them with the wrong information and yet they were here. Who were the others? There seemed to be at least four of them.

He hadn't time to consider the matter further because bullets were pouring down on him both from the opposite hillside and from Drugget and Quinn on this side of the cleft. He decided to try and circumvent the two gunnies by taking a little detour and getting up behind them. Taking great care not to expose himself to their sights, he slipped away, moving as quickly as his old limbs would allow. When he had gone a short distance, he became aware that the firing from the opposite hillside had dwindled. Taking advantage of the lull, Applejack scrambled forward. He was high and there was plenty of cover beneath the escarpment. Hugging the rock wall, he moved along it towards where he reckoned Drugget and Quinn were concealed. As he did so a rattle of fire nearby sent shards of rock flying into the air. Applejack ducked lower. He couldn't see where the shot had come from but he didn't think it was from either Drugget or Quinn. His first thought was that at least one other gunslick was somewhere in the vicinity, but then he remembered the lettering on the coach and it dawned on him that it was buckshot: could it be from the type of shotgun favoured by a Wells Fargo messenger? As if in answer, a figure briefly emerged from cover below him.

'Hold it right there!' Applejack snapped.

The man glanced up and for a moment Applejack thought he was going to swing the shotgun round and fire at him.

'If you're Wells Fargo,' Applejack called, 'I'm on your side. If I wasn't, you'd be dead now.'

The man hesitated for the fraction of a moment and then let the shotgun hang loose.

'I'm a Wells Fargo agent. From the look of you, I guess you must be Applejack.'

'The man we're after is somewhere on the hillside

up ahead,' Applejack shouted.

'You mean Drugget?'

'Yeah, and he's got someone with him.'

Just then two shots rang out, ricocheting from the rock wall above Applejack's head.

'There's his calling card,' Applejack shouted. 'Let's get movin'.'

They crept forward again, the Wells Fargo man moving parallel to Applejack and just below him. The boom of rifle fire on the opposite hillside had resumed and was now gaining in intensity. Applejack figured they must be getting quite close to where Drugget and Quinn had been positioned, but there had been no resumption of fire from them. Then, as the cliff face took a slight turn, Applejack saw a place where the rim had crumbled, giving relatively easy access to the top of the cliff. In an instant he realized that they must have slipped away to where their horses were tethered.

'Drugget's got away!' he shouted.

The Wells Fargo man climbed the intervening space to join him.

'Up there,' Applejack pointed. 'I don't think I can make it. You carry on climbin'. You might still be in time.'

The man nodded and began to ascend the rough scree. Applejack turned and started to clamber back down the rocky slope. Gunfire was still echoing around the hillsides but it had faded and as he got lower, it became sporadic. He looked up at the opposite cliff. Plumes of smoke still billowed but they were coming from high up; it seemed that the gunslicks up there had had enough and were making for their horses. Reaching the bottom, he began to move towards the stagecoach. He could see neither Cooley nor Baines but the man he had met at the Triangle S was still there together with the others who Applejack surmised were more Wells Fargo operatives. Occasionally one would raise his gun and fire but to all intents and purposes the battle had come to an end. As he approached the stagecoach he saw the figure of Baines descending the opposite slope. Accompanying them, his left arm clutched in his right, was Schandler. Applejack saw him and waved and in a few more moments they all met at the stagecoach.

'Hell!' Applejack said, 'I never expected to see you folks.'

'Good to see you, Applejack,' Baines said.

He turned to the man behind him.

'I think you've already met Chesterton,' he said.

The two shook hands.

'I told you Drugget's target was the bank at Gladstone Notch. How come you're here?'

'There ain't no bank at Gladstone Notch. We just put two and two together and came up with the conclusion that Drugget was more likely to attack the stage. It was an easy matter to telegraph Wells Fargo and arrange this set-up.'

'What happened to those gunslicks up there?' Applejack said, indicating the top of the hill.

'We got Schandler to thank for upsetting

Drugget's applecart. He's taken a bullet in the arm but he'll be OK.'

Schandler grimaced at the marshal's words.

'Seems Schandler and a few of the Triangle S cow-pokes who stayed loyal to him decided to take their chances and opened fire on Drugget's boys. That's right ain't it?'

Schandler nodded.

'It was enough to derail Drugget's plans.'

Applejack suddenly flinched.

'Drugget!' he said. 'Him and his right-hand man Quinn have got away! They got to the top of the cliff. Their horses were up there. One of the Wells Fargo agents climbed up after them but I think he was too late.'

'Not if Cooley's got anythin' to do with it,' Baines snapped. 'He's up there lookin' for Drugget now!'

Applejack had not been the only one to work out Drugget's position; observing the puffs of smoke coming from the nearer hillside and once catching a glimpse of the oldster, Cooley had guessed what was happening. Turning away from the battle which seemed to be going in their favour, he began to ascend the slope. It was hard going and in places he was forced to expose himself to the risk of gunfire, but after a struggle he had almost succeeded in reaching the crest when the wind carried an unmistakable sound to his ears. It was the sound of horses snorting and stamping as the diminishing sounds of gunfire disturbed them. He was struck with a new idea. He glanced along the length of the hill crest, determining whether to carry on with his intention of getting above Drugget or reaching the horses and loosing them. That way he might be able to prevent Drugget and maybe some of the other gunslicks from getting away and still be in a position to come back at him. Deciding on the fresh course of action, he hauled himself over the top of the hill and began to move quickly towards the sound of the horses. They weren't far off. He had taken not more than twenty paces before he saw them partly concealed among some bushes. He saw something else too. Just approaching from another direction was the outlaw leader himself with a gun in his hand. Cooley froze, uncertain whether Drugget had seen him or not. Drugget paused and glanced behind him; apparently he was unaware of Cooley's presence. As Drugget moved again towards the horses, Cooley stepped forward. The movement attracted Drugget's attention.

'Cooley!' he exclaimed.

'It's over,' Cooley began. 'Drop your—'

Before the words were out of his mouth, Drugget raised his gun and fired. The bullet whistled by Cooley's ear as he drew his own gun. Drugget was firing rapidly and Cooley felt a burning pain in his shoulder as a slug tore along it. He stepped slightly to one side and steadied himself. Resting his gun hand on his other arm, he slowly and deliberately squeezed the trigger. The gun jumped in his hand and, as the smoke cleared, he saw that Drugget's arm had dropped and he was looking down at his chest.

A dark stain began to spread across his shirt. He took a step forward, raising his head to look at Cooley. Cooley was about to fire again but something held him back. Drugget took another firm step and then began to stagger. His gun fell from his hand. Cooley advanced, his gun still pointing at Drugget. He was close enough now to read the dazed expression in Drugget's eyes. Blood was issuing from his mouth in a red trickle and his shirt was soaked. For a moment he seemed to recover and his features creased in an expression of hate.

'Cooley,' he said, but whatever message he was about to deliver remained unspoken. The dazed look returned to his eyes and his face seemed almost to melt as his legs gave way and he sank forwards to the ground. He twitched once, twice, and then lay still. Cooley took a few paces and knelt beside him. Carefully, he turned him over, but he already knew that Drugget was dead. He got to his feet and began to walk back towards the hill when he saw another man heave himself over the crest. He raised his gun but in a moment he realized that it wasn't one of Drugget's gunnies but one of the Wells Fargo operatives. The man looked at him with a startled expression.

'You should be more careful,' Cooley said. 'I might have drilled you.'

'I heard the shots,' the man said. 'What happened? Looks like you been hit.' Cooley became aware again of pain. He looked down at his shoulder. Drugget's bullet had creased the flesh but it didn't look serious.

'The man we're after is over there,' he said, indicating with his good arm where Drugget lay in the grass. 'He gave me no choice.'

The man's eyes swept the hilltop.

'Was there just one of 'em? The oldster said there were two.'

'Two?' Cooley repeated.

'Yeah. He mentioned the varmint's name. I think it was Quinn.'

'They left some horses,' Cooley said. 'He must have got away.'

When Cooley and the Wells Fargo man had made their way back down the hill and delivered their news, there was quiet satisfaction about the outcome as regards Drugget, but a gnawing sense of dissatisfaction that his right-hand man had been allowed to escape. Applejack cursed and Baines slapped the palm of his hand with his fist. The Wells Fargo men looked at each other.

'There's a chance!' Cooley suddenly exclaimed. 'Most likely he'll be headin' for the Triangle S. If we can turn this coach round we might be able to beat him to it.'

'Cooley's right,' Applejack snapped. 'There's a cut-off which might let us get ahead of him.'

'Come on, what are we waitin' for?' Chesterton said.

'What about our man?' one of the Wells Fargo agents said.

'We might be able to pick him up. If not, it ain't too far a walk to Gladstone Notch.'

Wasting no further time, they got aboard the coach, the Wells Fargo men inside with Chesterton and Schandler, while Cooley, Baines and Appleton took their places on top. Since he was the one who knew about the cut-off, Applejack took the reins. It wasn't easy to turn the stagecoach round. The horses were unsettled and nervous but at length they were pointed back the way they had come. The stagecoach moved slowly at first but soon began to pick up speed. As they moved, Cooley filled in Applejack with the details of what had occurred since the oldster had left him, while the oldster in turn outlined events at the Triangle S.

'I wasn't too sure about Chesterton,' he said. 'In the end I had to take him on trust. There was no alternative.'

They were bowling along at a rattling pace and as the coach bumped and lurched they had to hang on by their fingertips.

'Are you sure you can handle this thing?' Cooley said.

The oldster grinned and spat through the gap between his front teeth.

'I drove a stage before,' he said.

As if to back up his statement, he cracked the whip and at the sound, the horses strained harder in the traces. Suddenly the stagecoach swung to the left and the others were almost thrown clear.

'I guess this must be the cut-off,' Cooley drawled.

The coach hit a bump and once again almost sent them all flying. Applejack chuckled.

'Guess I should have warned you folks,' he said.

The coach had slowed a little, but not very much.

'Never mind your drivin' skills,' Baines said. 'Are you certain this is the cut-off? Don't seem to be much evidence of a trail.'

'Have faith. Just you concentrate on keepin' a lookout for that varmint Quinn.'

They hadn't gone much further when Baines drew their attention to a low cloud that had appeared to their right.

'What do you make of it?' he said to Cooley.

'Riders, but there must be more than one of 'em to raise that kind of dust.'

He leaned down and shouted through the window for the people inside to be on their guard.

'Looks to me like they're headin' this way,' Baines said.

Applejack looked across at the marshal.

'What do you want me to do?' he said.

'Keep right on goin',' Cooley replied.

For a short time the dust cloud seemed to move parallel to them and then it grew bigger. Cooley and Baines cradled their rifles. They could all see now that a big group of riders was coming towards them.

Applejack laughed.

'Hell!' he said, 'you don't think the coach is under attack by another gang of bravados?'

Cooley looked closely at the approaching riders.

'Not another gang,' he said. 'Just the same gang. Unless I'm very much mistaken, that's Quinn near the front.'

'Haven't they had enough?' Baines replied.

Cooley peered more closely and then leaned back. Baines glanced at him. His features were wreathed in a broad smile.

'What's so funny?' Baines said.

Cooley sat up again.

'Take another look yourself,' he said.

Baines leaned forward.

'You're right about Quinn,' he said.

'Yeah, but he ain't leadin' the gang in an attack. The gang is leadin' him. I'd say Schandler's boys finally got the better of their new foreman. I'd say they were bringin' him in.'

Applejack broke into a cackle.

'Jumpin' Jehosaphat, you're right. They got that skunk in as near a three legged cross-tie as I seen and still be able to sit on a horse.'

As the riders came up, Applejack brought the coach to a halt. One of the riders came forward.

'Howdy.'

Cooley nodded.

'We caught this varmint tryin' to meet up with some of his comrades,' the man said.

Quinn scowled and muttered something beneath his breath.

'We figured to hand him over to you. We can take care of what's left of the rest of 'em.'

The man lowered himself in the saddle and peered through the window of the stagecoach.

'You got Mr Schandler in there?' he said.

'Sure have,' Cooley replied. 'He's been injured

but it ain't serious.'

Just then the door of the stage opened and Schandler climbed down, followed by the Wells Fargo men.

'Get Quinn down off his horse and put him inside,' Cooley said. 'We'll take him back to Little Fork. I imagine Wells Fargo might want to have a chat with him.'

'I got plenty on Drugget and the rest of his gang that Wells Fargo are goin' to be interested in,' Applejack said. 'Enough to put Quinn away for a long time.'

Quinn was lifted from his horse and led to the coach. When he was inside, Cooley addressed Schandler.

'Ain't got nothin' on you,' he said. 'In fact, we owe you. Things might not have turned out the way they did if you hadn't intervened.'

Schandler nodded. A couple of his ranch-hands got down and assisted him into the saddle. Cooley turned to Applejack.

'OK, driver,' he said. 'I think our business here is about completed. Let's get goin' for Little Fork.'

Applejack cracked his whip and the coach lumbered forwards. The little group of Triangle S riders watched it as it picked up speed and then, at a signal from Schandler, started to ride away. Baines's eyes followed them till they had gone.

'You figure Schandler will be able to deal with what's left of Drugget's gunslicks?'

Cooley nodded.

'I don't reckon they'll hang around now that Drugget's dead. They took quite a beating back there.'

Applejack ejected a stream of saliva.

'Quinn deserved to go the same way as Drugget,' he said.

'He's got a point,' Baines remarked.

'No, it's better like this,' Cooley said. 'In the long run, gun-law ain't the answer. This way he gets to stand trial and come to justice.'

'Like I said, I got plenty on the whole gang,' Applejack commented. 'He's goin' to be lookin' at a long time behind bars.'

'That's for the circuit judge to decide,' Cooley said.

There was silence for a time. The stagecoach rolled forwards at a smoother pace and this time there was no danger of anybody being flung off. Cooley reached for his pouch of Bull Durham and passed the tobacco to the others to build smokes.

'You know that Chesterton is Belinda's uncle?' Cooley remarked.

'Is that so?' Baines said. 'She's gonna be plumb surprised to see him. Guess that means she'll be goin' back with him to Harpington.'

Cooley took a deep drag of the cigarette. The deputy marshal's words made him somehow think of the last occasion he had seen Belinda with the hatbox under her arm. He was looking forward to seeing that hat.

'I don't know,' he replied. 'Could be she'll decide

to stay in Little Fork.' Baines looked at him and a slow grin spread across his face.

'Looks like when you were lookin' for old Applejack, you found somethin' else besides.'

'You were lookin' for me?' Applejack said. 'Hell, I never figured I was lost.' He glanced at the others and they all laughed.

'You'll be headin' back to the Indian River to work that claim?' Cooley said. The oldster raised his whip and cracked it over the horses' heads.

'Wouldn't want to attract any no-good claim jumpers and owlhoots to Little Fork,' he said. 'It used to be a peaceful town. Maybe me and Suky will settle down and take it easy if it ever gets back that way.'